"Yo

Howard's voice was exasperated. "That's the simple truth, Belinda, but I don't like being questioned and I wish you'd drop it."

"Great in bed? So I'm great in bed, am I? How many boyfriends do you think I've had?" Belinda asked. "How many lovers? Go on, guess—do you think you're the fifty-first?"

"I don't know and frankly I don't care. What you did before you met me, that's none of my business."

"You're my lover, and that makes it your business. So let me tell you, Howard, you are the second."

There was an awkward moment of silence, then Howard stepped back muttering, "Oh, for heaven's sake!"

Belinda gulped. "No, that's not quite right," she said in a low unsteady voice, "I'd better change that. You *were* the second."

SALLY COOK lives in Norwich with her two small sons. She was a professional writer for nine years before she branched into romance fiction.

Books by Sally Cook

HARLEQUIN PRESENTS
1223—DEEP HARBOUR
1287—BELONGING
1320—HIJACKED HEART
1407—TIGER'S TAIL
1440—INHERIT YOUR LOVE

SALLY COOK

Spring Sunshine

Harlequin Books

TORONTO • NEW YORK • LONDON
AMSTERDAM • PARIS • SYDNEY • HAMBURG
STOCKHOLM • ATHENS • TOKYO • MILAN
MADRID • WARSAW • BUDAPEST • AUCKLAND

Harlequin Presents first edition October 1992
ISBN 0-373-11495-8

Original hardcover edition published in 1991
by Mills & Boon Limited

SPRING SUNSHINE

CHAPTER ONE

' "Parishioners at Lower Mumbling in Dunshire were shocked yesterday by the news that their vicar, fifty-one-year-old Frank Burberry, had eloped with——" '

'How about this, Belinda?'

' "The church organist, petite blonde mother-of-four Mary Ellison, thirty-one." '

'About what, Mum?'

'This advert. Drop that dreadful rag and listen a minute! "Botanist seeks secretary-assistant to work on book project. Must be available for field trip, one month in Crete, starting on the third of April; possibility of up to three months' subsequent part-time work. Applicants should be fast, accurate shorthand-typists with an interest in flowers." '

Jennifer Barford lowered her newspaper and beamed triumphantly across the breakfast table.

Silence, all around the table.

'So what about it?' Charmian, Belinda's younger sister, demanded.

'As a job for Belinda, of course! You did say you wanted a change, didn't you, darling?'

' "It's diabolical," said the vicar's son, twenty-two-year-old actor——" '

Belinda folded over the page, to stop herself reading any more. On Sunday mornings her brain wasn't at its most efficient: she had only been half listening to her mother.

'Well, yes. . .'

5

'Which paper's that, Jenny?' Graham Barford asked, peering over the top of the Sunday Times Business Supplement.

'Oh, it's. . .' much fumbling of pages '. . .Tuesday's *Melchester Chronicle.*'

'Tuesday's!' Belinda groaned teasingly. 'And I thought I was half asleep! Mum, you do realise that it's five days old? And that there are three Sunday papers here waiting to be read?'

'I picked it up by mistake—and it's just as well I did, because doesn't that sound fascinating?'

'Let's have a look.'

'About two-thirds of the way down the right-hand column.'

And there it was. 'Botanist seeks', et cetera. Plus a name, and a telephone number.

'"Dr H Henderson,"' she read out loud. '"Melchester 902137."'

'Rings a bell,' Graham murmured. '902. . . Oh, it's the Plant Research Unit up at the University.'

'Most likely,' Belinda agreed. 'So who knows H Henderson?'

She'd have been willing to bet somebody would: it was a family joke that, between them, the Barfords knew everyone in Melchester. And, sure enough, Charmian's brief frown brightened into a triumphant grin. 'It's Howard Henderson, of course!'

'So who's he when he's at home?' asked her mother.

'I don't think you'd know him, Mum; or Lindy either. He was at the Briggses' party a couple of months ago, that one I went to with Alastair. We had a very interesting talk in the kitchen, all about wild flowers. His life's work is to measure how many there are in different places, or something.'

'Millions, I should think,' Belinda said with a grin, 'so that should take him a week or two. Well, what's he like, Char? The ideal boss?'

'Actually he could be. I'll tell you one thing, Lindy— he's absolutely gorgeous! Fair-haired and hunky. Joanna Clark was going bananas over him.'

'But do you think it's worth following up?' Jennifer persisted.

Belinda wasn't seriously job-hunting; she hadn't even got as far as flicking casually through the classifieds. It was true, though, that she had been saying all weekend that she was fed up with Mr Browning and Cornwell Electronics. Fed up with London, come to that: recently she had been popping back home to Melchester more and more often. Just the evening before, her mother had suggested that a local job might suit her better, and she had agreed that it mightn't be such a bad idea.

Boring, though: bor-ing! She had gone to London in the first place because she wanted to live a little, to explore the wide world outside Melchester. All right, it hadn't been an unqualified success, but if she did give it up she wanted to do something reasonably exciting next, not to come back home to Mum and Dad and settle into a dull job in some solicitor's or accountant's office up the road.

Crete sounded pretty exciting.

Crete! Sun and sand, lazy meals in cheap tavernas, the warm blue Mediterranean. A botanist for a boss— and a gorgeous botanist at that—instead of greasy Mr Browning with his dandruff-flecked suits. Yes, that was definitely worth following up!

'Could be,' she agreed, not imagining for a moment that her family would be fooled by her pretend casualness.

'What was the starting date?' her father asked.

'April the third. And it's—gosh, it's March the second today! That's torn it. It's no good—I'd have to give a month's notice at Cornwell Electronics.'

'Resign tomorrow,' Jennifer offered.

'How could I? Even if I phoned up tomorrow, I'd hardly be offered this job on the spot, would I?'

'I suppose not, but if you didn't get it something else would be sure to come up pretty soon. There are lots of secretarial jobs in the *Chronicle*, and you've got a year's experience now, so you'll have no trouble landing one.'

'That's a point.'

'And if you do get caught between jobs we'll help you through for a month or two, won't we, Graham?'

'I dare say so,' her father agreed dutifully.

'You're going for an interview dressed like *that*?' Jennifer yelped when Belinda came down for breakfast the following Wednesday.

'That's the idea,' Belinda agreed.

'It won't do, Lindy.'

Belinda glanced down at her bright blue cotton blouse, bright red woollen skirt, and her cardigan, which was a rainbow of thin, uneven multi-coloured stripes. Half a dozen colourful papier mâché bangles looped her arm, her fingers were weighted down with her collection of silver and enamel rings, and round her neck was a gold chain, inset with little enamelled medallions, that Jennifer and Graham had brought her back from their holiday in Bali the previous year.

'It's perfectly tidy,' she said defiantly.

'Not exactly sober, though, love.'

'The University isn't Cornwell Electronics—thank goodness! Remember Annie said she put on a smart suit for her interview, and she was interviewed by a guy in jeans who fell about laughing at the sight of her.'

'But that was to study, love, and you're going for a job.'

'Quite a special job.' Belinda grinned. 'Look at it this way. If Dr Henderson doesn't like me looking like this, we're not going to get on, and it'll be no good my working for him.'

'That's a point, but I'd still rather you off-loaded some of the hardware.'

'I'll think about it,' Belinda said absently, reaching for a glass of orange juice. She didn't want to do it, though. It felt like a release from prison, not going to work for Mr Browning on a Wednesday morning, and she relished the chance to dress as she chose for once.

In big ways Belinda had never been rebellious, but she did like to get her own way over little things. She put a lot of thought into her outfits, and she was used to laughing off her mother's endless grumbles that she had about as much dress sense as a typical two-year-old.

'You'll need to leave in ten minutes,' said Jennifer, glancing at the kitchen clock.

'It won't take me half an hour to get to the University, Mum.'

'You'd be surprised. It's not the easiest place to find your way around.'

Curse it, her mother had been right, Belinda realised forty minutes later, as she hurried down the umpteenth identical-looking concrete walkway. Late already!

Not easy to find your way around? That was the understatement of all time. Melchester University was a maze, a mess, a positive rabbit warren. All the buildings and all the walkways looked the same, and she could swear that she'd been along this one twice already!

No: this wasn't European Studies yet again; it was Environmental Sciences, the little sign said. And the porter had told her to take the second left at Environmental Sciences, and then she couldn't miss the. . . Wonder of wonders, she'd found it!

She hurtled through swing doors, up a flight of stairs, and there was Room 1.12, with a little plaque announcing that it was the office of Dr H Henderson.

Only three minutes late. Not what she'd been aiming at—she didn't want to give Dr Henderson the impression that she was chronically unreliable or, worse, not too fussed about his job—but still not a total disaster.

She took a deep breath and knocked.

No reply. She waited a moment, then knocked again. And again.

It had to be the right room. He couldn't have given her up after three minutes. Was he on the phone, perhaps? Or. . .

Cautiously she turned the handle and eased the door inwards.

It opened on to a smallish box-shaped room. One long wall was lined with crammed bookshelves, and down the other were arranged a grey metal filing cabinet, a chair, and a grey metal desk with a large notice-board above it. A couple of other chairs completed the sparse furnishings, and at the desk the only occupant was sitting—he had his back turned towards her and was writing furiously.

'Morning,' Belinda said in a sunny voice.

The man at the desk started, then rapidly spun round

towards her. A pair of clear grey eyes, set under heavy brows, caught hers and held them.

'Who on earth are you?' he growled.

Oh-oh! Gorgeous wasn't the word she'd have used. It implied something weak and harmless, while this man had all the tense, agile strength of a wild cat. And, like a wild cat taken by surprise and cornered, he had his claws out already!

'Belinda Barford. Your ten o'clock interviewee. For the secretarial job. You *are* Dr Henderson?' she finished, her voice growing more and more uncertain.

'Yes, but you're——'

He eased back the sleeve of a grey sweatshirt to look at his watch, and Belinda took advantage of the momentary pause to say, 'Not *very* late.'

'Oh,' said Dr Henderson. 'I could have sworn it was about half past nine.'

'Well, just finish what you're doing. Don't mind me.'

Dr Henderson's glare implied that that would be no easy task. His brows lowered, and Belinda, suddenly conscious of her flamboyant appearance, wondered for a moment if she was going to be dismissed as unsuitable without even an interview.

Not quite. 'Don't interrupt me,' he said tersely, and turned back to his desk.

Wasn't that just charming? Belinda thought to herself. Charmian might have mentioned that he was as boorish as he was beautiful. Even Mr Browning had showed her a lumbering sort of gallantry, but it didn't look as if she was going to get much of that from Dr Henderson.

Still, he hadn't told her to leave. She tiptoed into the room, past him, and slung her shoulderbag over the back of one of the spare chairs. She glanced around the room, but took in little more than she had done orig-inally, because Dr Henderson acted on her attention like a powerful magnet on a bunch of iron filings. Even when he was ignoring her, she could hardly tear her eyes away from him.

He wasn't a particularly big man. His shoulders were broad, but he looked to be slim-hipped, and he certainly didn't carry any excess weight. She wouldn't have called him short, but he was no giant: at a guess, he'd be a little under six foot standing up. Fair hair, longish and straight, brows a couple of shades darker, and film-star-type craggy good looks: square jaw, long nose, well-shaped mouth and those penetrating grey eyes. His clothes—well-worn grey cord trousers and matching sweatshirt emblazoned with a rainbow and a Greenpeace slogan—didn't grab the eye particularly, but there was no need for them to, when they were wrapped around such a spectacular hunk of a man.

Really, he was a bit *too* handsome, she thought critically. He wouldn't need to practise his charm any too hard in order to get women flocking his way!

He sighed, turned a page, tapped his Biro on his desk. And Belinda, conscious that it wasn't good tactics to stare at him for too long, dragged her attention away, and towards the notice-board above his desk.

Half of it was crammed with official-looking notices which did nothing to hold her attention. The other half was a lot more interesting, though. On it was pinned a series of photographs of wild flowers.

Lovely flowers—and lovely photographs too, she decided, bending over to look at them more closely. They were all thoughtfully composed, well lit and per-fectly focused. If these were Dr Henderson's, he defi-nitely knew how to handle a camera.

'When you're ready.'

'Oh. Sure,' she said hurriedly, drawing back and sitting on the nearest chair. 'Hey, you didn't come on the last Whale Walk, did you?'

'The what?'

'The Whale Walk, last summer. All along the coast. It's a regular thing, a sponsored walk in aid of the Save the Whales campaign. I saw the Greenpeace slogan, and I thought maybe you'd have. . .'

'No, I didn't.'

'That's a pity, you'd have enjoyed it. There was a really good bunch of us—we had a fantastic time. I went around my office and the neighbours and got nearly two hundred pounds in sponsorship. Mind you, I had some terrible blisters by the end, but it's all in a good cause, isn't it?'

'That's true,' Dr Henderson agreed in a bleak voice.

'Well, as I was saying, I'm Belinda Barford.'

'So I see.'

'And I do think your photographs are marvellous! Those colours! Did you take them yourself? You must be a very good photographer: it's not easy to do really close close-ups like that. Are they from Crete?'

'No, they're not. And if you'll forgive me saying so, Miss Barford, I had the impression that it was I who was to interview you, not vice versa.'

Oh-oh! Claws out again! Belinda gave an apologetic smile, put her knees together and her hands on her lap, and said cheerily, 'Fire away, then.'

'Thank you.' Dr Henderson paused. The pause drew out, and out, as his steely gaze pursued a leisurely inspection of her. She gave him a a bright smile, but she got no indication in return that he liked what he saw.

She didn't really doubt that he did, though. Just about

everybody warmed to her sunny nature, and almost every man she met lavished compliments on her pretty face, her misty-fair curly hair, her bright blue eyes and her neat figure. It didn't look as if Dr Henderson was the effusive type, but surely he was delighted to be offered such a personable assistant?

'You're twenty, you said, Miss Barford?' he queried.

Inspection passed? It had to be!

'That's right, twenty-one in June.'

'And you have a diploma in secretarial studies from Melchester Polytechnic.'

For the next five minutes he took her through the details of her short career, and as she replied to his questions Belinda's confidence began to rise. Maybe the interview hadn't begun ideally, but she felt sure she would get the job. And why not? She had never yet gone after a job that she *hadn't* been offered!

Her achievements weren't the kind to make headlines, but they were certainly nothing to be ashamed of. She'd been a prefect and captain of the tennis team at Melchester Comprehensive. She had passed a few exams, for all Graham's grumbles that she could have done better if she'd put her mind to it; had gained goodish marks for her secretarial diploma; and she'd done well at Cornwell Electronics, with a promotion to senior secretary halfway through her year of working there.

And a generous dose of enthusiasm was put into her replies, as she began to get the measure of Dr Henderson. She wanted to work with him. She very definitely wanted it.

All right, he wasn't the smoothest-mannered charmer she'd ever met, but she surely wouldn't find it too hard to rub away his prickles. She liked his manner, calm and confident; she liked his looks; she liked his quiet, deep voice. What a pleasure it would be to have a boss she looked forward to joining for work every morning!

Dr Henderson made a few notes on the pad of paper in front of him, then moved on to ask about her personal life. He soon discovered that she was single and free to travel, and that she was planning to give up the flat that she shared with three other girls in Wandsworth, South London, and move back to Melchester to live with her parents for a while.

'Do you have to give much notice to your flatmates?' he asked her.

'A month as from Monday—the same as my job.'

'From Monday? Last Monday? So you've already resigned?'

'Yes, I have.'

'Could I ask why?'

'Because I want this job!' She couldn't help laughing at his taken-aback expression. 'No, really,' she went on, 'I'd been planning to leave my job anyway. I don't like living in London as much as I'd expected, and I've been there just over a year, so I've given it enough of a try. I've been thinking of resigning for a while, but I needed a prod to make me actually do it, and when my mother saw your advert in the paper, that was that! I thought, if I don't resign straight away I'll mess up the timing and have no chance of getting it. Not that I'm taking it for granted that you'll take me on, because I'm sure you've had an absolute avalanche of applicants.'

She smiled winningly, and tried not to take it amiss when Dr Henderson didn't smile back. 'So if you don't pick me,' she carried on, 'I'll give myself a couple of weeks' holiday and then look for another job locally.'

'I didn't name the salary in my advert,' Dr Henderson

said coldly, 'but perhaps I should warn you that it isn't especially high.'

'I guessed that—but I'd love to go to Crete! And I love flowers, and I think I'd enjoy working on the project with you, which is the main thing, after all.'

'You love flowers. Then could I ask you what this one is called?' He pointed at a photograph near the bottom of his notice-board.

'Looks like a buttercup to me,' Belinda said, standing up and moving closer to look at it. 'Look, Dr Henderson, don't get me wrong. I do love flowers, honestly, but I'm not pretending to be an expert in them. I didn't do much biology at school, and I don't know all the botanical names or anything.'

'Obviously not. That's actually *ranunculus brevifolius*, so it's not even in the same family as the common buttercup.'

'Oh. Well, I'm very willing to learn.'

'I'm glad to hear it,' Dr Henderson said. He frowned. Then he went on, in a decidedly cool voice, 'I'll be frank, Miss Barford—you're not the type of applicant I'd envisaged taking on for this job. I'd have preferred somebody a little less—er—*dramatic*. But your qualifications are adequate, and, as you point out, time is running short. I'd previously appointed somebody who was forced to withdraw through ill health, and, contrary to your expectations, I haven't received an "avalanche" of applicants for my repeat advertisement. So I'm prepared to offer the job to you.'

'Well, thank you!' Belinda retorted with heavy sarcasm.

Dr Henderson appeared not to notice her tone. 'I trust you realise,' he continued, 'that we'll be in Crete to work? It won't be a holiday, Miss Barford. I tend to work long hours on field expeditions, and I'll need you to accompany me each time, to take notes and act as driver.'

'What do you think I imagined, for heaven's sake? That you'd pay me to spend all day lolling around on the beach?'

At that, he did have the grace to look a tiny bit abashed. 'I'd just thought I ought to make it clear what's involved,' he responded. 'My research is very important to me, and my budget's tight, so I can't afford any setbacks. The last thing I need is a clock-watching assistant who grumbles if I don't finish the day's work dead on time.'

'You'll see from my references that I'm not one of those,' Belinda assured him. But her earlier enthusiasm had disappeared entirely, and she didn't make any attempt to bring it back. Gorgeous hunk, indeed? Humourless prig was more like it! She'd burnt her boats now, and she wasn't prepared to refuse the job, but it was only too clear that it wasn't going to turn out to be the ideal assignment of her dreams.

'There will be a few days off, naturally,' Dr Henderson said in a more conciliatory tone. 'But there's also some preparation I'd like you to do before we leave. Will that cause any difficulties to you?'

'What kind of preparation?'

'Reading, mainly. My research is about the effect of pollution on the wildflower population. I've been pursuing it ever since my schooldays, but now I've almost finished, and the book I'm writing is partly drafted already. I'd like you to read through the text I've written before we set off.'

'Just one book? That's no problem.'

'I'll print the material out on my word processor, and send it to you. At your parents' address?'

'I'll be going back to London tonight, but I could pick it up there at the weekend.'

'That should do admirably.' He managed a smile this time: a broad smile that crinkled the corners of his eyes and showed off very white teeth.

Gosh, was he gorgeous! A little *frisson* of sexual awareness slithered down Belinda's spine and, following it, a shiver of uncertainty. She wasn't used to men who affected her the way this one did, and she wasn't used to men who were so obviously immune to her in return. All her first ideas about how she'd handle Dr Henderson seemed to have been way off beam—and she'd just committed herself to spending a whole month with him, a long way away from home. She would have to hope her second attempts at finding a way to handle him were a whole lot more successful than her first had been.

Maybe reading his book would give her some clues. Or if not she'd have to ferret out some more information about him from elsewhere, she decided as she rose to her feet, because she certainly didn't intend her month abroad to turn into an ordeal.

'I'll be in contact over your employment formalities and the travel arrangements,' Dr Henderson said seriously.

'Of course. You can always leave a message for me at my parents' house. I'll look forward to starting work with you.'

'I trust so.'

Rather to her surprise, he held out his hand. And after a moment's hesitation, she took it. His grip was cool and firm, but there it was again, that little shiver of physical awareness that he stirred in her.

Cool it, Belinda, she told herself. You're keyed up, that's all. But all the same, it was with oddly mixed feelings that she began to retrace her steps to the University lodge and the road home.

'So there'd be just you and this Dr Henderson?' Jennifer asked dubiously over supper that evening.

'As far as I could gather. It's a small-scale research project, not like a major archaeological dig or something.'

'That does sound a little——'

'Oh, *Mum*! I'm not a child any more—I can look after myself. And he's certainly not interested in anything more than a working relationship with me, I can assure you.'

'What makes you so sure?'

'His attitude, his manner—everything. Mum, I can tell when a man's interested in me, and that one isn't.'

'But you're interested in him?'

'I might have been,' Belinda admitted frankly, 'if he'd reacted differently. You know it's a while since there's been anyone special in my life, and I don't want to stay alone for ever. And he's got the sort of looks that would make any woman turn for a second glance—and a third! But honestly, his keep-off signals were so clear that I'd be stupid to even hope for anything to develop. And maybe that's as well, because you're right—it is an unusual situation, and I wouldn't want things to get out of hand.'

'Quite right,' Graham said quietly. 'Even so, I think I'll just ask around and see what I can find out about him.'

'Dad!' Charmian groaned.

'No, Dad's right, Char. I'd like to know all I can before I'm plunged into the deep end!'

The following two days at Cornwell Electronics seemed to drag endlessly. Then it was Friday, and back to Melchester—and the promised pile of typescript.

A huge pile at that, a good three inches thick, enough to make Belinda's spirits sink. But she needed to make a good impression on Dr Henderson when they next met, so she refused a suggestion from a friend that she go to a disco that evening, and settled down to read it instead.

It was quite interesting in places, but she had to admit that, written in dry academic language and larded with pages of statistics, it wasn't ideal light entertainment. She couldn't help being impressed by the weight of Dr Henderson's learning, though, and reading his work did fill in a few gaps in her understanding of his research.

Crete wasn't the only place where he had researched, she discovered: it seemed that he generally went on three or four field trips each year to different European destinations. And he'd been to the island three times, at five-year intervals, with this to be his fourth visit. Assuming he had been sixteen or seventeen the first time, that would make him around thirty-one, which tallied with her first impressions of him.

It tallied with what Graham had learned too, from a cautious chat with Jock Watson—Professor Watson, head of the Plant Research Unit—over a round at the golf club. 'Turns out your Dr Henderson's a high-flyer,' he told her. '"Very solid," Watson called him, and coming from Jock that's quite a compliment.'

'That's good. But I'd hardly call him *my* Dr Henderson, Dad.'

'He's not anyone's, from the sound of it. He's a bit of a loner, Jock said. Works long hours and lives alone.'

'Not even a girlfriend?'

'Can't say I asked,' Graham chuckled. 'But I must say my mind was put at rest, Lindy. It doesn't sound to me as if he's your type at all.'

'I guess not,' Belinda agreed. And laughed; but under the laughter she recognised the note of faint wistfulness in her voice. What *was* her type, after all? She had never been short of admiring men, but men *she* admired were infinitely harder to track down. Really, Paul, her boyfriend during her last years at school, had been the only serious man in her life—boy, rather. Dr Henderson was a man, but Paul hadn't been in the same league at all—and that had been a friendly rather than a passionate affair.

She had never made it a top priority to replace Paul after he had left Melchester to go to Leeds University, and they had amicably agreed not to wait for each other. Her life was very full of family and friends and various activities, and she had assumed that the right man would come along in his own good time. She had no interest in pursuing a relationship with anybody who wasn't absolutely right for her. But several of her friends had recently become engaged, and she couldn't help being conscious of the fact that she was a little unusual in still being completely alone at nearly twenty-one.

She hadn't even come close to falling in love. So many of the men who asked her out struck her as shallow and immature, lacking in energy and enthusiasm—one-dimensional characters. Mentally they bored her, and physically none of them had affected her—well, the way Dr Henderson had affected her, she admitted uneasily to herself.

And that was what she was looking for: a man who could make her pulse race and her heart thump, a man she could admire and look up to. But of course he would have to fall in love with her in return, and she was level-headed enough to realise that even a face as pretty as hers wouldn't guarantee her the love of that kind of a man.

Nothing could. You can't hurry love, that was the truth of it. And so she'd just have to wait patiently, and make sure she enjoyed life in the meantime.

Over the next few days Belinda finished reading the typescript, checked her passport, and packed her case according to Dr Henderson's instructions: lightly, with casual clothes only, for a Cretan spring climate that would be rather like an English summer, with warm daytime temperatures and cooler evenings.

At last her final day at work came—and went—and at seven a.m. on Monday she found herself standing in the hallway of her parents' house waiting for Dr Henderson to collect her.

He appeared dead on time. And, in spite of all her resolutions to be businesslike and coolly friendly, her heart gave a little jump at the sight of him, looking casual but devastating in a thigh-hugging pair of blue denims and a white shirt under a blue sweatshirt.

All right, she wasn't his type, and perhaps he was too reserved a character to be hers, but in so many ways he was just the sort of man she was looking for. Intelligent, successful but without ceasing to be concerned about his environment, physically attractive: wouldn't it be won-derful if one day she found a man just like him who did fall in love with her?

Sure it would, she reminded herself cheerfully, but

hadn't she better forget the passion for now, and concentrate on building up a decent working relationship with this man?

While he loaded her suitcase into his car, she hugged her parents and Charmian goodbye. She turned to him again to find him peering suspiciously at the black box she had slung on a strap from her shoulder.

'Is that a tape recorder?' he demanded.

'It's a Walkman.'

'There's no need to bring it. I don't like dictating into machines, and you have reasonable shorthand, don't you?'

Belinda couldn't help laughing. 'It's not for work, for heaven's sake! It's to play music. No way could I survive a month without my favourite tapes.'

'You're planning to play pop music on *field trips*?'

'Why on earth not? The flowers won't mind, will they? Though actually they won't hear it, and nor will you, unless you particularly want to. I have a very good pair of earphones.'

'I'm glad to hear it.' He opened the passenger door for her, and Belinda, after a final, final round of goodbyes, slid into the seat next to him.

'Why,' she exclaimed, 'you're a right one to complain about *my* pop music! How many tapes do you have here?'

'Quite a few.' He half smiled as he eased the car through its gear changes. 'Play one if you want to.'

Did he mean it, or was he testing her consideration? Why should he? He must like the music himself, or it wouldn't be in his car! Belinda took him at his word, rifling through the collection that crammed the dashboard shelf and the map pocket on her door. Finally she selected a Bruce Springsteen album, and soon rock music was blaring at full volume through the car and out of the half-open windows.

'Good stuff, this.' She had almost to shout to make herself heard above the music. 'Haven't heard it for ages. You're a real hard rock fan, aren't you?'

'That and reggae, mainly, but I prefer rock to drive by.'

'My stuff's poppier. I really like Madonna. Do you like her? And Kylie Minogue, and Rick Astley?'

'Can't say I do.'

'You don't have to look so disapproving. Everyone to their own.'

'I didn't mean to,' he told her.

He had done, all the same, as if he thought her taste was for unacceptably light and insubstantial music. But she tried not to dwell on it: she just settled back to enjoy the music.

It was little more than an hour's journey to Gatwick Airport, and with fairly light early morning traffic they had a smooth, fast journey. Soon they had parked the car, off-loaded all but their hand luggage, and found seats side by side in the departure lounge.

Dr Henderson—Belinda meant to call him Howard, but she hadn't had a chance to call him anything yet— had kept his portable computer with him, and once they had bought coffees he settled down to show her how it worked. Fortunately she'd used a similar model before, and though she warned him that she'd take a week or two to build up to full proficiency she rapidly got the hang of the basics.

When he turned the keyboard over to her she success-fully started a word-processing document without any prompting, and she was rewarded with an only slightly grudging, 'Well done.'

'I'm not just a pretty face, you know,' she teased him in return.

'I've no doubt you're more than that.'

He smiled at her, a wide white smile that took in his eyes as well as his mouth. Belinda found that it did some very strange things to her insides.

Idiotic! Sheer chemistry, that was all. Most likely he had that effect on every woman. What was it Charmian had said about Joanna Clark? All right, he lived alone, but he maybe spent a lot more time out with women that he spent at home.

Not your type, Belinda, she told herself firmly. A humourless prig, remember?

But she couldn't help hoping he'd turn out to be a lot less humourless, and a lot less priggish, before the month was out.

'Well,' she said, 'if that's the end of lesson one, how about telling me a little about yourself?'

She settled back into her airport chair, expecting a lecture that would last until their flight was called. After all, Dr Henderson would be a very unusual man if his favourite subject of conversation wasn't himself! But she soon discovered that she was wrong about him once again. His smile faded rapidly, his eyes left hers, and after a casual remark that he 'really didn't like talking about himself', he reached into the pocket of his denim jacket for a paperback.

Oh. Cool it, Belinda, she reminded herself. Not everybody's as chatty and forthcoming as the Barford family.

'What's the book?' she asked.

He tilted the cover towards her so that she could read the title, then opened it at page one.

'*Clueless in Eden*,' she read out loud. 'Looks like a really good murder story.'

'I expect it will be.' He turned past the title page and began to read the first chapter.

'I like murder mysteries too. Any chance of borrowing it when you've finished?'

A grunt.

Oh. Very definitely the man who'd only taken her on because he hadn't time to find a more suitable assistant. Enough ventured, nothing gained. She had brought a paperback herself, so she retrieved it from her bag, and settled down to join him in reading until the flight was announced.

A three-and-a-half-hour flight and a three-hour time difference meant that it was mid-afternoon by the time they emerged from the plane at Heraklion Airport on Crete. It was a warm afternoon, with a sparse scattering of clouds scudding across a bright blue sky. A bare fifty yards from the runway, the Mediterranean sparkled in the sunlight.

'Mmm, doesn't that look tempting?' Belinda sighed. 'I could just peel off my clothes and——'

'Wait till we get to our hotel, at least!'

She didn't need to glance at Dr Henderson to know that this time at least he was amused rather than exasperated with her: the warm note in his voice made that clear enough. And though she had had no more luck in prising him away from his novel during the flight, she was so elated to have arrived on the island that his stand-offish attitude didn't mar her own good temper.

'So we'll be staying near the sea?'

'For the first few days we are. I've already booked us into a hotel, in a small resort only twenty minutes' drive from here.'

'That's good—but why just a few days? It isn't a big island, is it? Surely we won't need to move base at all?'

He shrugged. 'As islands go it's a fair size, and not all the roads are up to British standards. I'm reckoning on us having five bases, first here, then to the east, then the west, but even then we'll spend a lot of time driving.'

'I hope you've hired a comfortable car.'

'It'll be a Seat Marbella. You can't expect a Ferrari on an academic research budget! It's not luxurious, but it's reliable, which is the main thing. How's your skill at tyre-changing?'

'Rusty!' she laughed. 'And I hope it'll stay that way.'

'So do I, but I'd advise you to check the spare and the jack before we get going tomorrow.'

'Oh, come off it, Howard! You only get punctures every once in a blue moon.'

He raised his heavy brows a fraction, though she wasn't sure whether it was the 'Howard' or her casual attitude to punctures that had earned her this. Or both, perhaps, but his only comment, calm and serious, was, 'They're remarkably common out here.'

'So how's *your* tyre-changing skill?'

'You're the driver. And a Women's liberationist, I'd have thought?'

'Not that much of one!'

She said this quickly, lightly, then bit her tongue. She'd have to do better than that if she was going to find a way to win him round. 'And *I'd* have thought,' she went on, still teasingly but rather more thoughtfully, 'that you'd be far too gallant to sit by and watch while a lady struggled! But there's no need to worry: I've been through a car maintenance class, so I should be able to recognise the jack and put it to good use.'

'I'm glad to hear it.' He smiled, and reached out a

hand to touch her arm as they approached the terminal building. 'I'm a reasonable mechanic myself, but you'll doubtless do some driving without me while we're here, and I wouldn't like to see you stranded on a Cretan mountainside.'

'Nor would I,' Belinda assured him. And in spite of his oblique warning that she'd be expected to pull her weight, it was he who got behind the wheel as they left the airport. They were both tired, as he pointed out, and as he knew the roads he'd be the fastest at getting them to their hotel.

CHAPTER TWO

FROM the balcony of her hotel room Belinda could see sand: empty sand, a long, long stretch of it, leading down to the even emptier expanse of the sea. By British standards it was a hot day, but there were less than half a dozen people sunbathing, and nobody at all was swimming.

I bet the water's cold! she crowed to herself. She heaved her suitcase on to the bed and threw it open. It was only a moment's work to extract a tiny bikini, white with pink spots, a pink T-shirt dress to wear over it, a pair of slip-on sandals and a beach towel. Soon she was ready to try the sea for herself.

She paused outside Howard Henderson's door, but he had closed it with such finality a few minutes earlier—after naming six-thirty as the hour when they would meet for supper—that she didn't like to knock. Is he the type who unpacks everything straight away? she wondered. Or will he be standing on *his* balcony, watching me run across the sand and plunge in the sea?

Maybe he'll come and swim too.

As soon as she stepped off the concrete of the hotel terrace she slipped off her sandals—and almost squealed at the heat of the sand. Running made sense—it stopped her toes from toasting. A few yards from the sea she threw down the sandals and the beachbag containing her towel, heaved off her dress and tossed it on top of them, and dashed towards the water's edge with hardly a pause.

29

It was cold! Cold, cold, cold! And the beach shelved
so gently that she had barely reached thigh-depth
before the chill of it became enough to bring her to a
halt. She paused for a moment, wondering if this was
sheer lunacy, then took a deep breath and plunged
under the water.

Still cold. Still absolutely freezing. She did a dozen
rapid strokes, turned on to her back, paddled a little,
admitted to herself that it wasn't fun at all, and gave up.

As she waded on to the shore she glanced upwards.
The white slab of her hotel, punctuated by windows and
festooned with balconies, was right in front of her. Her
room was on the second floor. She scanned the balconies
and saw a few small figures, but she was too far away to
be sure if one of them was Howard.

Pity he hadn't come down. It would have been more
fun swimming with him. With him to encourage her, to
laugh at the coldness, she'd most likely have stayed in
the water much longer.

Ah, well. He was her boss, not her boyfriend, and she
couldn't force him to come and swim with her. She
waved at the second-floor balconies just in case he was
standing there, then reached for the towel, spread it over
the hot sand, and flopped down, dripping, on top.

It was hard to believe the sun could be so hot, even at
five o'clock, and the sea so cold, but while the quick
swim had been a penance, sunbathing was a delight.
Soon she was dry enough to anoint herself with suntan
oil. She wasn't used to putting it on by herself: usually
she had somebody to do her back. She glanced up
towards the balconies again, but she couldn't see any
sign of movement on them. He couldn't have come on to
the beach without her noticing—there were so few
people around.

Oh, well, at least she'd be eating supper with him. Sunbathing wasn't an occupation that demanded company. She reached round to her back to unfasten her bikini top, arranged her arms and legs so she'd tan evenly, and drifted off to sleep.

'Belinda! Belinda!'

'Not yet,' she muttered sleepily. 'Can't be time yet.'

'It's twenty-past six. Time to stir, Belinda.'

Surfacing slowly to wakefulness, she felt herself shiver. It wasn't as warm now: maybe a cloud had crossed the sun. She half opened her eyes, and what she saw made her jump into a sitting position. Some cloud: this one was called Howard Henderson.

A relaxed Howard at that, claws definitely retracted, and smiling down at her in a way that more than made up for the failing sunshine. She grinned back at him in sheer warm pleasure, sat back a little—and realised that her bikini top was falling off!

'Oops,' she said cheerfully.

'Let me do that.'

'Thanks.' She turned her back to him, and felt his cool hands take the straps out of hers. His fingers brushed lightly against her bare back as he fastened the catch. And was it her imagination, or did they creep round to linger momentarily on the side of her breasts before reluctantly drawing away?

And she'd thought he didn't fancy her!

Calm down, Belinda, she reminded herself. It was hardly the world's most enthusiastic response, considering how much of her was on display! Come to that, it wasn't remotely her style to strip down to try and stir a man into showing some interest. The only kind of interest she wanted to encourage was the kind that came from men who appreciated her mind as well as her body.

Which Howard certainly didn't, to judge from the way in which he'd promptly withdrawn a couple of paces from her. 'As I was saying,' he went on, 'it's six-twenty already. I thought you'd maybe like a chance to shower and change before we found somewhere to eat?'

'I'd certainly better,' she agreed, hurriedly folding the towel and gathering her things together.

'You mustn't leave it too late to shower, or try it first thing in the morning. The water's solar-heated, and it soon cools down after dark.'

'I'll remember that.'

He bent to take her beachbag, and Belinda scrambled to her feet, looping her sandals over her hand. Barefooted, she was a good head shorter than him. She would have enjoyed walking next to his ruggedly handsome figure, and being conscious of a few second glances from tourists drinking on the terrace as they approached the hotel, if she hadn't had the sensation that he was somehow trying to distance himself from her.

Was he embarrassed because of her momentary display of toplessness? Bother that! Lots of women on Mediterranean beaches went topless all the time, so the quick flash of breast that he'd glimpsed was hardly the scandal of the century.

She left him in the bar, and dashed up to her room. He'd have to wait rather more than ten minutes for supper, since she liked to take her time about getting ready, but she didn't dare to keep him waiting *too* long.

The water in the shower was pleasantly hot, and she lingered till she'd seen off every trace of brine and suntan oil. She washed her hair too, rubbed the dampness out, and gave it a five-minute burst from her travelling hairdryer, just enough to make it stand out from her head in a fluffy pale cloud, since the air was now too cool for it to dry naturally.

No tan yet, she mourned, slipping on a scoop-necked white blouse and a peasant-style print skirt, but it was bliss to be back in summer clothes, and not to have to wear tights. A cross-section of her jewellery collection, two shades of grey eyeshadow, blusher, red lipstick, a generous splash of duty-free Arpège—and a quick final check in the mirror to reassure her that she was looking good.

Pausing at the door to the hotel bar, she could see Howard propping up the counter, tapping his foot and glancing at his watch.

No need to rub it in, she thought: it was only just past seven. It wasn't her fault if he hadn't taken the same trouble with his appearance as she had taken with hers. In fact, it was definitely his failing. All right, he looked good in jeans, but he might have benefited from a shower and change after the journey.

He glanced towards the door just then, and she hesitated for a moment, conscious that her blonde prettiness would be set off perfectly by the dark wood of the door surround, before moving across the room to join him.

At closer quarters he looked cool and fresh, and he smelled faintly of a minty aftershave. Her first impressions had been wrong: he'd certainly showered. And—yes, he'd changed too, but from one pair of jeans and sweatshirt into another, almost identical.

'You bring lots, do you?'

'Lots of what?'

'Pairs of jeans and sweatshirts.'

She thought for a second that she'd been too familiar,

teasing almost, and that he'd bring his claws out in response, but fortunately he was relaxed enough to take it in good part. 'Only a couple of each,' he told her. 'I've packed a couple of white shirts too, then I have denim shorts, khaki shorts, half a dozen T-shirts—oh, and a pair of swimming trunks.'

'You obviously don't go in for pinstriped suits.'

'On a *field trip*? I shouldn't think there's a taverna in all Crete for which you have to wear a tie.'

Maybe not, but he'd look good in a suit, she thought to herself. And even better, most likely, in swimming trunks. Would he swim with her tomorrow? He would surely enjoy a dip after a hard day's work.

'What are you drinking?' he asked coolly.

'Orange juice, I should think.'

'You wouldn't prefer an ouzo? Or a gin and tonic?'

'No, thanks. I'll have some wine when we eat, but I don't like to drink a lot.'

When he'd ordered it, and another ouzo for himself, he turned back to her and said, 'You bring lots too. Of jewellery.'

'Always, yes. Nothing too precious, in case of accidents, but I don't feel dressed without some on.'

'You'd look better without as much.'

Belinda blanched. All right, she thought, I dressed to please myself, not you, *sir*! No point in trying to please you, is there? It's an impossible task.

But she kept back her irritation at his little criticism, and said in a cheerful voice, 'Maybe, but I like it! It's fun choosing clothes to wear and jewellery to go with them. I really like rifling through my collection and picking out necklaces and chains and rings and bangles and things. And though none of this is valuable, it all means something to me. See this ring here, on my middle finger? My sister gave me that for my birthday last year. And this little silver and turquoise one I bought on holiday in Majorca, and. . .'

Taking advantage of his silence, she continued to chat on about her jewellery for several minutes. She guessed it wasn't the subject he would have chosen, but she didn't want to drop it and risk floundering around in the search for common ground with him. At least while she was talking they gave the impression of being at ease together, however false it was.

And false it certainly was, at least on her side. She couldn't relax in the slightest with Howard next to her.

She was so acutely physically conscious of him. She couldn't take her eyes off him. It was the most she could do to avoid staring at his face, and force them to roam, though they lingered everywhere, enjoying the sight of the long-fingered hands cradling his ouzo glass, the forearms exposed beneath the rolled-up sleeves of his sweatshirt, the powerful thighs that his denims wrapped so closely. Indeed, if she hadn't been working to hold herself in check she'd have been sorely tempted to do more than enjoy looking: to reach out and touch him.

Heavens, this man got to her! She had admired plenty of attractive men before, but she'd never known one to affect her like this, making her so nervous that she was babbling away like a halfwit, making her mouth dry and her hands itchy. And it was such a cruel irony that it should be this man, when anyone less interested in her she could hardly have imagined!

He didn't even seem concerned to make his share of the conversational effort, and when she had exhausted the subject of her jewellery they fell into a silence so uneasy that she soon broke it again, speculating lightly about the other people in the bar: why they were in Crete, where they came from, and so on.

Howard slowly seemed to revive and contribute a little more to the conversation, and the atmosphere between them was a tiny shade lighter by the time he eased himself off his barstool, saying, 'We won't eat here, unless you particularly want to. I know a little taverna up the road which does some good local dishes—or did, five years ago.'

'Sounds fine.'

'Did you bring down a jacket or cardigan?' he asked. 'I don't want to drive after drinking, so you'll need one for the walk back.'

'I'll just go and grab one.'

She dashed to her room, checked her make-up in the mirror, turned out her case and unearthed a fluffy pink mohair cardigan from the heap of contents, then dashed down again.

Howard, wearing a denim jacket over his sweatshirt, was waiting for her in the hotel foyer. His hand just touched her back, guiding her, as they passed through the swing doors and began to walk up the main street of the little resort.

In five years it had changed considerably, as he was soon forced to confess. Though he had found their hotel, one of the oldest on that stretch of seafront, with no trouble, the same wasn't true of the taverna he remembered. He shook his head at the bar-restaurants lining the main street, where a smattering of tourists sat eating and drinking, and the only restaurants in the side-streets they checked out weren't yet open for the summer.

'I really don't mind where we eat,' Belinda assured him. 'We're both tired, and I could eat just about anything, anywhere, right now.'

'No. I want to take you somewhere special.'

'Why?'

Her thoughtless query sparked an interrogative look from him. Belinda quailed. Why, when you don't like me? was what she had meant, but she didn't plan to say that out loud.

Fortunately he didn't press the point. 'Hold on,' he said. 'Over there's a sign to the harbour. I remember a good place down there: let's just see if it's still around.'

The road to the harbour was narrower, little more than a dirt track. But a bare five hundred yards down it opened on to a tiny bay, part sand and part rock, in which a couple of fishing boats rocked at anchor.

And there at the head of the bay was an old-fashioned taverna, with a group of Cretan fishermen sitting drinking on the terrace.

'Clever you!' Belinda exclaimed. 'It looks perfect. But are you sure they'll do food?'

'I'm sure they will.' Howard shepherded her inside, and it was immediately clear from the mouthwatering smell of herbs and fresh fish and lemon that he was right.

'You've been to Greece before?' he asked.

'Only once, and then we stayed in a big hotel complex, so I've only ever eaten in a couple of tavernas.'

'Well, the thing to remember is that the menus in all these places are virtually identical, but the food that's on offer is often quite different. There are generally one or two dishes of the day, even in the quiet season, and in fish tavernas what's available depends on the day's catch. So the best way to pick your supper is to go to the kitchen and see what's going.'

Belinda didn't need further encouragement to make

for the archway, largely blocked by a big refrigerated display, that led to the kitchen.

'There's swordfish, see, and sardines,' he said, pointing them out, 'and lamb kebabs, and something in that pot on the stove. Is it moussaka?' he continued, turning to the waiter who had silently approached them from behind.

'Moussaka tomorrow, sir. That's macaroni pie. Little bit like moussaka, with meat sauce and cheese topping.'

'I'll have the pie. Belinda?'

'Swordfish, I think.'

'And we'll have some of those prawns, grilled, please, to start with, and a Greek salad, and a carafe of red wine. OK?'

'Fine,' she agreed, a little fazed by the way in which he had taken command.

'Let's sit on the terrace,' said Howard.

They took a table at the far end from the fishermen, and soon their wine arrived. After a long wait bread and a Greek salad, with tomatoes, cucumber, raw onion and feta cheese, followed it.

It was surprisingly companionable to sit together, eating salad and bread dipped in the oil and lemon dressing. They didn't talk much, just sat listening to the soft slap of the waves against the rocks and the boats.

Soon it grew dark. A trickle of other holidaymakers arrived, and a tape of Greek music began to play inside the taverna. Howard laughed.

'What's so funny?'

'Everything else changes, but never that. *Zorba the Greek*—hear it? At every taverna in Greece they seem to play the same half-dozen records year after year.'

'I'd have thought they'd play rock music these days,'

she remarked. 'Paul Simon and Dire Straits and that kind of thing.'

'In Spain, yes, and Italy, but not in Greece.'

A moment later the waiter reappeared with the prawns, which were delicious, and they had barely finished them before he brought the swordfish, garnished with the inevitable tomato and chipped potatoes, and a huge portion of macaroni pie.

Belinda ate till she was bursting. She drank steadily too, feeling relieved as the thick Cretan wine began to ease away her tension, and barely noticing when Howard called for a second carafe.

This was the life! OK, it wasn't a holiday, and she was willing to bet he'd work her hard tomorrow, but the taverna, the bay, the food, all made this a glorious place to be. OK, Howard was her boss and not her boyfriend—and a pretty reluctant boss at that—but in the shadows of the terrace she could almost forget that, and simply enjoy gazing across the table at him.

Leaning back on his chair, wine glass in hand, a halfsmile on his face as he looked back across the table at her, he seemed a different man from the austere Dr Henderson who had interviewed her. Just as handsome, with his strong-boned face deeply shadowed in the faint light that came from inside the taverna, but far more approachable. She had called him Howard a dozen times now, and there had been no hint from him that she was being over-familiar.

Over coffee she told him a silly story about her and Charmian's attempts at water-skiing on their last visit to Greece, and he laughed in response, and told her a story about *his* scuba-diving. Maybe it was just the wine, but they seemed to have no trouble finding common ground now. She was beginning to lose the uncomfortable feeling that he didn't like her, didn't approve of her, and to settle back into her usual easy self-confidence.

Once or twice he smiled and held her eyes, and she was hard pressed not to believe that he was coming to like her very much. Could the intense current of attraction that she felt really be one-way only? Wasn't it possible, she asked herself, that Howard felt it too?

But he'd been so off-putting earlier!

Well, it wasn't so hard to explain that, she thought hazily. He could hardly have come on too strongly to her in an interview. A man had to watch the way he behaved towards his assistant. He wouldn't want to be accused of sexual har. . .haruss. . .somehow, her fuzzy mind just couldn't bring up the right word.

It was almost eleven by the time he finally paid their bill. Belinda's foot slipped momentarily as she made her way down the wooden steps from the terrace to the beach, and Howard reached out to take her arm. Then he slipped his arm right round her as they moved towards the track that led back to the town and the hotel.

Nice. More than nice. It was like completing a circuit and feeling a warm current of pleasure run through her. This wasn't sexual ha. . .whatever, this was pure and simple lust.

The track was dark and bumpy, her head was muzzy from the wine, and Howard's body, as she leaned against it, felt hard and warm and comforting. More than comforting, arousing. She gave a little murmur of pleasure, slipped her own arm under his and around him, and squeezed him close till they were walking with thighs touching.

There was a sweet inevitability about it when they

drifted to a halt. Howard drew her, firmly but gently, into the shadow of a half-built building. For a moment she gazed up into his face, hazily expectant, and then his mouth descended upon hers.

She responded without thought, without doubt, without anything but sheer delight as his arms tightened around her, and his kiss slowly deepened. She was right! He did like her. He did want her!

And she wanted him—but how! Her lips parted eagerly under the insistent pressure of his, and a stronger current of pleasure trickled down her as his tongue invaded her, gently but insistently exploring the soft cavern of her mouth.

How perfect he felt! It was like coming home, but to a place infinitely thrilling, infinitely enjoyable. He was just the right height: tall enough to make her feel enfolded and possessed, but not so tall that she had to strain upwards to sustain the kiss. Her arms just fitted over him and around his neck. Her fingers explored the pleasurable contrast in texture between his hair and the smooth skin at the back of his neck. Her breasts, crushed against the broad expanse of his chest, seemed to have acquired a few million more nerve-endings.

His mouth slowly eased away and, panting slightly, she buried her face in the hollow of his shoulder. He smelled of wine and lemon and minty aftershave, a warm clean inviting smell. One of his hands crept down to her hips and moulded her lower body to his.

'You are the most disgracefully desirable woman I've ever met,' he whispered in a low, thick voice.

'You too. Man,' she whispered back, none too coherently.

'You want me, don't you?'

'Yes. Oh, yes!'

Oh, yes, keep doing that, her fuzzy mind urged, as his fingers brushed aside her cardigan to expose her collarbone. He bent his head and dropped a line of little kisses along it, just above the neckline of her blouse.

Belinda felt as if she was melting. A hot sensation seemed to be flooding through her, and focusing deep inside. Her breasts had swelled till they ached at being confined within their skin. She wanted his mouth to drift lower, lower, to find and caress them. Her fingers scored restless lines through his thick fair hair.

What bliss! What delight! It was everything she had wanted and hadn't expected to happen. It was a surprise and a pleasure and a glorious relief, and she wanted it to go on and on.

'We'd better get back to the hotel,' Howard murmured into her ear.

She didn't want to move, didn't want to leave the shadows. But Howard was already easing away from her, taking her hand and pulling it gently, and she wasn't in a state to resist him.

They wove back along the track and down the main street, arms wrapped around each other. Her head kept dipping over to nestle against his shoulder. He kept stopping to kiss her again, lightly but urgently. The walk seemed endless, and yet it seemed to take no time at all. She waited, flushed and happy, by the lift as Howard retrieved their room keys from the reception desk.

'Your room?' he asked, once they were cocooned in the lift and moving upwards.

Her room? They oughtn't to go there, she thought hazily. It would be an invitation for too much to happen, too fast. But she didn't want to leave him yet. She wanted to hold him again, be kissed by him again, and there wasn't anywhere else for them to go except to his room.

'Howard, I don't. . .' she murmured.

'Here we are,' Howard said confidently. He checked the number on the door key, and unlocked the door.

Belinda was blearily aware of the mess that confronted them. Her suitcase was on the floor and the clothes she had up-ended out of it were strewn across the bed. Her damp bikini was in the washbasin, and the hotel towels and her own beach towel were jumbled on the floor of the little shower-room. But what was all that, when Howard had her in his arms again, and was kissing her again, deep, drugging, urgent kisses that drove every other thought out of her head?

Every touch of his hands, his mouth, his body, sent fireworks of desire shooting through her. She felt weak with desire, to see him, touch him, feel his flesh against hers, satiate this heavy hollow longing that filled her.

He shrugged off his jacket, and through the thin material of his shirt she could feel the rising heat of his body. He unbuttoned her blouse, punctuating each button with a short fierce kiss on her mouth. He guided her on to the bed, and in the same movement found and released the catch of her bra. She felt his hands take the weight of her aching breasts, and his thumbs seek out and caress her swollen, straining nipples.

When he bent his head to them, and the heat of his mouth closed over the areola, it was all she could do to keep from thrashing on the bed, the prickling desire his flicking tongue aroused was so intense. As if sensing her frustration, he brought the weight of his body to rest on her legs, pinning her, and let his hand roam possessively down the soft swell of her stomach.

When his fingers moved still lower, and found the

damp eager core of her, she felt a momentary panic. This was bliss, but she hadn't meant things to go so far, so soon. She opened her mouth to protest as his fingers slid into her, but the feelings he aroused were so incredible that all she could manage was a faint moan.

She hadn't believed it was possible to feel like this, blind to everything but this unbearably vivid longing. To hell with caution—she had to have him, had to possess him, had to bring their mutual desire to consummation. She reached for him with hands and legs, eager to pull him closer, to feel his body touching hers at every point. But he was in control, and he wouldn't let her hurry him. His mouth moved downwards, and his tongue traced up and down the valley of her groin, finding points of agonising sensitivity beneath the soft skin.

She bucked against him, driven to the edge of desperation, and he moved his arms to pin her to the bed, keeping up the relentless movement of his tongue.

Desire and frustration seemed to build up in waves within her. She wanted this to continue, and yet she wanted more, more! It was glorious to feel his strength, his control, to enjoy his skilful playing on her senses, but it was agony not to have him take her now.

Her longing crept to the edge of the absyss of unbearableness, and hovered there, and found a fine balance that held her there. Her struggles against him slowly subsided, and she concentrated on the intense inner feelings that his caresses were arousing in her.

She had ceased to fight and was almost beyond tension by the time he loosed his hold of her and hurriedly threw off his few remaining clothes. There was just a moment when she could drink in the sight of his finely muscled

body, and then he moved closer again, and poised
himself above her.

He held himself there for a long, an unendurable,
instant. She tried to catch and hold his eyes, but he was
lost in in intense concentration. Then he met her gaze
briefly, intensifying the shock as he plunged deep inside
her.

The ripple of her inner fulfilment came, and faded in
the agony of his withdrawal, and was restored, and then
she was lost in sheer pleasure, caught between the
rhythm of her inner tremors and the deep counterpoint
of his movements.

Whatever level of ecstasy he took her to, there always
seemed to be another peak, and another, still to be
scaled. Then his rhythm caught and failed, and for a
moment she was floating free, conscious only of the
sensation of clutching at him in a blind hot convulsion
of bliss.

And he was collapsing, a warm, sweating, living
weight on her, his breath coming in hoarse pants like
her own.

It was several minutes before she could trust her voice
enough to even whisper, 'That was wonderful.'

Howard slowly eased himself away from her, and fell
on to his back by her side. 'Pretty good,' he agreed. He
turned to her, ripe with the satisfaction of a male animal
who has had his fill. 'Mmm, you're lovely.' He reached
out a hand and ran it, casually, with none of the
absorbed concentration of his caresses a few minutes
earlier, down the curves of her side. 'And you should
sleep now, or you'll never make that early start in the
morning.'

'I will.' A great surge of tiredness was already beginning to wash over her. She thought of sliding under the

thin counterpane, but she hadn't the energy to make even that minimal movement. Hypnotised by contentment, she watched Howard heave himself off the bed. Her eyes drank in the lines of his lithe body, gleaming with sweat, as he padded across the floor to the shower-room. Then she closed them in satiated exhaustion as he disappeared behind the door.

It was an effort to resurface when she felt him taking hold of her shoulders and easing her into a sitting position. 'Here,' he said. 'Drink some water, or you'll get dehydrated in the night.'

'Must I?' Belinda protested sleepily. For answer he curled her fingers around the cool smooth shape of a glass. She drained its contents, let him take it out of her hand, and reached out to pull him down beside her.

He resisted, easing himself out of her clutch as she subsided on to the pillow, and bending down to loosen the bedcover and drape it over her. 'Sleep well,' he murmured. And if he said any more, she didn't hear it.

Knock, knock. Pause. Knock, knock. Curse it, who could it be? Why wouldn't they go away?

Belinda turned over lazily in bed and reached out a hand. It met nothing but the empty space between coverlet and mattress.

Vaguely she sensed surprise, and sat up—too suddenly. Her head didn't seem to be in its usual place, and she had to put a hand to it to stop it spinning. Her forehead was hot and damp.

Oh, gosh! Howard. Wine, too much wine, and Howard. She remembered now. She turned to survey the expanse of double bed, and took in the fact that he was definitely there no longer.

Knock, knock.

'Yes?' she croaked.

'Belinda?' Howard's voice called through the door. 'It's seven-thirty. Breakfast time.'

Curse breakfast. Curse Howard. Up already, by the sound of it, and as disgustingly chirpy as a morning blackbird.

'Belinda, are you awake?' he persisted.

'Sort of.'

'I'll see you downstairs in twenty minutes. I want us to be off by half-past eight.'

Twenty minutes! Was he kidding? Maybe not, she decided, hearing his footsteps fading away down the corridor, and after a moment's painful thought she stumbled out of bed and into the shower.

Ouch! She'd forgotten Howard's warning that the water wasn't warm early in the morning. It was marginally, but only marginally, hotter than the sea had been the previous afternoon. Not what she would have chosen, but at least the shock of it did something to clear her head, and she certainly wasn't tempted to linger under the jets.

She dressed speedily in a shocking pink sunsuit, one of her favourites, with a skimpy top that stopped at her midriff, and an equally skimpy skating skirt. Worn with fat white beads and big white button earrings, it made her look fresh and lively, even if she didn't yet feel it. Strappy high-heeled white sandals completed her ensemble, and she dashed downstairs only ten minutes late.

She saw Howard as soon as she entered the dining-room, sitting at a window table, and looking cool and disgustingly healthy in a white T-shirt and khaki shorts. He wasn't looking her way, and she had a moment to pause and enjoy the sight of him.

Heavens, what a first day it had been! And what a

first night! Rash was hardly the word for it, she thought guiltily. That wasn't her normal style at all. It had taken her well over a year of regular dates with Paul before she'd been enticed into bed with him, and she'd never been persuaded into any other man's bed.

But then no man had made her feel like this before, rawly alive and excited and nervous all at once. No man had ever awoken that kind of sensuous longing in her before. Her rashness hadn't been entirely the effect of the wine. Sober and hung over the morning after, she was still crazy about Howard.

Perhaps she shouldn't have done it, but she couldn't feel sorry, standing there gazing her fill of him. If he felt the same way about her, it had surely been inevitable that they would be lovers before long. All they had done was speed up the process—and when it had worked out so wonderfully there was no cause for either of them to regret it.

Howard looked up and saw her, and she grinned at him.

In return, she got a sudden, devastating flash of smile, and then, to her surprise, it faded into a definitely more sober expression—in fact, one not far removed from a frown.

Was his head fighting back like hers, perhaps? No wonder. She couldn't have drunk more than half a bottle of wine the previous evening, and he must have put away twice or even three times as much.

'What a strain to wake up!' she said, half joking, half sympathetic, as she claimed the chair opposite his. He had already ordered for them both, she noticed—not that there was much choice in the simple meal of rolls, jam, fruit juice and coffee. 'Is this my cup?'

'You plan to go on a field expedition dressed like that?' queried Howard.

For a moment she just stared at him. He wasn't the only one with a pounding head, and if she could manage to be cheery in spite of hers he might have done the same!

But it wouldn't have helped to snap back at him, so she shrugged and smiled, and said easily, 'Why not? The sun's shining; it's going to be another lovely hot day. This is surprisingly comfy for driving in. And don't you make out that I'll frighten the flowers, because I won't believe you!'

'Those shoes won't do for a start.'

'I'm not planning to drive in these. I've a pair of espadrilles that I'll leave in the car all the time.'

'You'll wear the espadrilles all day.'

'*Please*,' Belinda added, in the voice her mother had always used to her and Charmian when they forgot to say it. 'Anyway, I won't. I like these shoes, and I can walk several miles in them if I need to.'

'Oh, for heaven's sake!' he groaned. Take them if you must, but you'll soon see that they won't do.'

It was a strain to hold her smile, but she was determined not to wreck their first morning with a squabble. 'Howard, darling,' she said, reaching for a roll and a plastic carton of apricot jam, 'I may be a brilliant typist, but I'd better warn you now, mountain climbing isn't my thing. Anywhere I can't go in these shoes, I'm simply not going.'

Howard gave her a contemptuous look. Abruptly, he pushed back his chair and got to his feet. He checked his watch ostentatiously. 'It's now five-past eight. I'll see you by the car at half-past.'

'I'll be there.' She gave him a final bright smile. It

would have been nicer if he had stayed while she ate her
breakfast, but perhaps it would be as well if he didn't, if
he was going to be such a grouch.

Was he always bad-tempered in the mornings? She'd
have to work out how to sweeten his mood, since she
certainly didn't want to suffer sulks and squabbles over
the breakfast table *every* morning! And she didn't want
them to continue any further into the day, so she'd better
eat up quickly, she reminded herself, and make sure that
everything was perfect when they met up at the car.

CHAPTER THREE

BELINDA arrived at the car at eight twenty-nine. She was still wearing the offending white sandals—on that point she was determined not to submit!—but in one hand she dangled her espadrilles, which were red, and clashed horribly with her sunsuit. Her sunglasses were pushed up on to her forehead, and over her shoulder was slung her beachbag, into which, after a rapid trip to the tiny supermarket on the corner opposite, she had packed a couple of oranges, a bag of fruit jelly sweets, a large bottle of water, a shorthand pad and a couple of sharpened pencils, and her handbag. The hand which steadied this load also held the rim of a newly purchased straw sunhat.

This evidence of her careful preparation was lost on Howard, unfortunately, since he wasn't there. Had she picked the right red Seat Marbella? She glanced around the hotel car park, and saw him emerge from the hotel entrance and stride towards her.

He too was heavily laden, with his camera bag, a clipboard from which a selection of papers flickered in the faint breeze, and what looked to be a small hamper.

'What's in that?' asked Belinda.

'Lunch.'

'That's good. I'd meant to ask you at breakfast whether you wanted me to arrange anything, but you didn't say, so I'd thought you maybe expected us to find a taverna.'

'There aren't any near my first site.' Howard fished

51

the car keys out of his jeans pocket and unlocked the tailgate.

Very efficient, Belinda thought, as he stowed away the hamper. Not very romantic, though. Not a word or look to acknowledge what had happened the night before. She could see that he might be concerned to establish himself as her boss as well as her lover, but he didn't have to go quite so far!

He unlocked the passenger seat, tossed the keys across the roof, and got in the car. Belinda claimed the driver's seat, slipped on her espadrilles and checked over the controls.

Reverse wasn't marked on the gearstick. They were bumper to bumper with another car in the car park, and she hadn't thought to check where it was when Howard had been driving. She waggled the stick a little but wasn't sure that she'd found it.

Howard was engrossed in a map of the island, liberally marked in red and blue pen.

'Up and left? Or down and right?' asked Belinda.

'What?'

'I have to reverse out of this parking spot.'

'Women!' He reached out to the gearstick, grabbed her fist, shifted it and the stick, and said, 'That way.'

'Thanks.' She smiled brightly and tried to catch his eye, but he had already returned to inspecting the map.

'So where do we go?'

He took a pen from the clipboard and made a note on a piece of paper clipped under the map. 'The Heraklion road,' he said, without looking up. 'I'll direct you after that.'

'To where?'

'Into the interior. It's almost due south from Heraklion, about forty kilometres from here.'

'Doesn't it have a name? Or is that a state secret?'

'No, it doesn't.' At least her persistence persuaded him to look at her, but with a harassed expression. 'It isn't a village, just a patch of wild flowers.'

'Show me on the map?'

She leaned over and peered at it, heard Howard take a sharp breath. *Oh-oh!* She'd already seen that he could be brusque, but she'd hoped that their lovemaking would have changed that—and instead it seemed only to have made it worse. Was he being cagey this morning because he now regretted their speedy leap into bed? Well, she didn't want that! She wanted him to decide, as she had done, that they had done the right thing, albeit a little too rapidly.

She was hoping that if she persisted he'd be chivvied out of his taciturn mood, and she'd judged it right, fortunately, because he let out the breath in a faint sigh, and said in a comparatively patient voice, 'It's just here.'

'Where you've put the red cross? Near T-s-a-g-a-r-a-k-i?'

She made a joke of her clumsy pronunciation, and Howard gave a short grunt of laughter. 'It's pronounced Sagga-rah-key.'

'Thanks, boss.' He grinned.

'Can we get going now?'

'Give me a kiss first.'

He stiffened momentarily, and for a moment she thought he'd refuse. But then she found his deep grey eyes and held them, and she knew she'd won. He paused for a second more, then reached over and just touched her mouth with his.

It was the sort of kiss he would have given to a child, not remotely erotic, but she'd made her point, and she felt much more light-hearted as she settled back into her seat and started the engine.

Luckily she found all the gears, reverse included, on her first try. It felt funny driving on the right-hand side of the road. She hadn't done it before, and if Charmian or her mother had been sitting next to her she'd have joked about her nervousness, but she didn't like to do that with Howard. It wouldn't do to seem to be taking advantage of their personal relationship, so she wanted to come across this morning as a really efficient and obedient assistant.

Anyway, she needed to concentrate on getting accustomed to the unfamiliar pattern of controls, and before she was relaxed enough to chatter they were in the outskirts of Heraklion, and surrounded by heavy traffic.

It took all her concentration to follow Howard's directions through a spaghetti of roads that were signed to Knossos, but to her pride she managed it without missing a single turning or prompting even one hoot from another driver.

The traffic was less dense once they were free of the town, and she ventured a sideways glance at him. He'd lowered the clipboard now and was gazing out of the window.

'I've heard of Knossos,' she said. 'Isn't that King Minos's palace?'

'That's right,' he agreed. 'So you know something about the Minoan ruins?'

'Not much more than that. I read a book about it years ago, and I remember a bull and a labyrinth, but it's all rather vague in my mind.'

'You've got that right,' Howard assured her. 'Though the archaeologists have never found a labyrinth like the one in the myths. Do you remember the story of Theseus? He was the prince of Athens who offered to be one of the youths chosen as tribute to the Minotaur, the terrible half-bull, half-man who lived at the centre of the labyrinth.'

'And Theseus killed the Minotaur, didn't he?'

'Sure did, and ran away with the princess afterwards. It's a glorious tale. Mary Renault wrote a couple of books which retell it superbly. Maybe we'll be able to track down English copies here if you'd like to read them.'

'You've read them yourself?' asked Belinda.

'Before I first came to Crete—and re-read them several times since.'

'So you really like that kind of stuff?'

'If it's well done. I find it fascinating to see how the ancient legends and the archaeologists' discoveries mesh together. The frescoes that have been found don't show anything quite like the Minotaur, but they do show bulls, and men and women doing what seems to be a kind of dance with them. . .'

He went on to describe some of the famous Minoan frescoes to her, and some of the other discoveries which had helped to build up a picture of the long-lost civilisation that had once existed on the island. He was clearly knowledgeable; and, what was more, he was enthusiastic. Most of Belinda's earlier attempts at conversation seemed to have fallen on stony ground, but she'd hit rich soil this time, and he became so engrossed that he almost forgot to tell her in time to turn off the Knossos road.

Grinning, Belinda took the turning with a screech of tyres. She was enjoying Howard's tales, but it was even more of a pleasure simply to see him so animated and forthcoming.

Perhaps he was used to living and working alone, and inclined to prickle in company, but he surely didn't have to be like that. She was becoming convinced that with a little patient drawing out he'd be the best of company.

He continued to tell her about the Minoan civilisation as she drove on, first up a good but narrow metalled road, then up an even smaller road. Then she rounded a bend to find that just the other side of it the tarmac surface suddenly ended, and the road degenerated into a dirt track littered with stones and pot-holes.

It took a squeal of protest from the brakes, but she managed to stop on the last foot of proper road surface. She lurched forward slightly in her seat, and Howard, who hadn't been watching the road, lurched further forward and had to put out a hand to save himself.

'Oops!' she said cheerfully. 'Looks like we slipped up somewhere.'

'What did you stop for?'

'I can't turn round without stopping, not without warning and on a narrow road like this. We'd better take another look at that map.'

'This is the right road.'

'Howard, you're not blind, are you? This isn't a *road* at all!'

'I did warn you the Cretan roads were bad.'

'Bad? Bad! That wouldn't even pass muster as a farm track!'

'There are worse roads than this on the island. Just take it gently. Keep to around twenty kilometres, and try to steer round the biggest pot-holes.'

'You mean I'm expected to drive over that?'

The rotter, he smiled! 'That's the general idea,' he said sweetly. 'And do try not to puncture the tyres.'

Belinda gritted her teeth and put the car back into first gear. From there she got it into second, and at a snail's pace they bumped and bounced across the stony, uneven surface.

They had been climbing steadily since they had left Heraklion, but soon they began to climb more rapidly, and the road started to curve around the sides of the mountains in an alarming series of hairpin bends.

'Stop a minute,' Howard said suddenly.

'There's nowhere to stop.'

'Here will do.'

Exasperated, Belinda slammed on the brakes and the Seat shuddered to a halt.

'What if another car comes?'

'Back a little further away from the bend.'

He waited until she was in reverse, then said in a more conciliatory voice, 'Actually, it's not likely. There's very little traffic on these roads. If a car does come we'll do what we would have done in any case, which is to reverse until we can find a passing place.'

'Most people have more sense than to drive along tracks like this, I suppose.'

This grouch didn't really merit a reply, and it didn't get one. Belinda backed about twenty yards, then stopped again. Howard got out of the car and set off back down the track.

Bewildered, she loosed her seatbelt and swivelled round to watch him.

It was a desolate spot. The mountainside rose steeply above them on one side of the road, and sloped even more steeply away on the other. No houses were in sight. And Howard was bending over, apparently peering at some rocks at the side of the road.

She had no idea what he was about, but it was a

pleasure to be released from the jolting of the car, and to sit there watching him. His fair hair gleamed in the bright sunshine. He moved with a lithe, unselfconscious grace that reminded her once again of a wild cat, and a contained purposefulness that assured her that he was confident in his surroundings, and sure of whatever he was doing.

Of course: he was looking at the flowers. She hadn't really noticed them herself—she'd been concentrating so fiercely on the driving—but now she could see that most of the ground was covered in a pink shrub that looked like aubrietia, and that there were clumps of other flowers, pink and yellow and white, all around the rocky outcrops.

Howard straightened up and came back to the car. He reached in through the open window for his camera case, and smiled at her. 'Come and see what I've found,' he said.

His animation was boyishly open and infectious. If he'd been enthusiastic about the local ruins, he was obviously ten times more so about the local flowers! He opened the car door and held out his hand, and Belinda took it as she wriggled across the passenger seat and out of the car.

Howard led her back to the outcrop, and drew her attention to some tall, rather spiky pinkish flowers growing in the patch of stony soil behind it.

'*Orchis Italica*,' he said proudly. 'Isn't it lovely? A classic example of the family *orchidaceae*. See, each of these spiky flowers looks a little bit like the body of a man.'

'So it does.'

'It's not tremendously rare, but I've never seen it on Crete before.'

'How clever of you to spot it!'

'I'm watching out all the time. That's why I leave you to do the driving.'

'Makes sense,' Belinda assured him.

'I'll just take a few snaps for the record, then we'll be on our way.'

She knew a little about photography herself, but Howard clearly knew quite a lot more. He checked the light, varied the exposure, even slipped a sheet of dark-coloured card behind the blooms so that he could photograph them in isolation. Everything he did with patient skill. Just like the way he had made love to her, she thought suddenly, and with that thought, and the sight of his strong body, bare-legged and bare-armed under the hot Cretan sun, she felt positively weak with lust.

Howard, absorbed in his task, obviously wasn't letting his thoughts take the same path, but his earlier gruffness seemed to have dissolved with the rising sun. He turned a brilliant smile on her once he'd finished.

'Back on our way,' he said cheerfully.

'Is it much further?'

'Maybe another five or six kilometres.'

'All over track like this?'

'Pretty much like this.'

'I see what you meant about punctures.'

He laughed, then said, more gently, 'Shall I drive for a bit? It's tiring, I know.'

'True, but I can manage, and you certainly can't trust me to spot a rare orchid at fifty paces!'

'You're doing fine.' He transferred his camera bag to his left hand and slipped his right arm around her shoulders. He hugged her, tightly, and she would have hugged him back, but he was pulling away again almost before her body had registered the gesture.

Still, she was pleased. Whether it was his hangover fading or his reserve thawing, now he was setting a much better balance between boss and boyfriend!

The five or six kilometres of road to the flower site took another half hour of driving, all of it wearing, since the road continued to swoop and dive around the mountainsides. The sun was now high in a cloudless sky, and for most of the time there wasn't another human being in sight. Belinda wouldn't have called it blissful, not when her rear was being bashed purple against the driving seat and her hands were aching from gripping the wheel, but her glimpses of the scenery were enough to tell her that Crete was undeniably beautiful in its harsh, remote way.

Goats grazed on the mountainsides, and when she peeped down into the valleys she saw terraces on which olive and orange trees were planted in neat rows.

They passed one small village, a cluster of houses and a church set back off the dirt road, and a few minutes later they approached another. 'This is Tsagaraki,' Howard said, a few moments before Belinda saw the Latin-script sign for herself. 'There's no need to stop. The site's on the other side of the village.'

The road was still twisting and turning, but soon they came to a spot where the ground levelled out on either side of it. 'Pull off the track,' Howard commanded. 'Not far, just to clear it.'

'You're sure this is the place?'

'Quite sure, but I'll check for my markers in a minute.'

The car lurched to a halt, and with a sigh of relief Belinda switched off the engine. It was unexpectedly quiet. They were out of sight of the village, out of range of its goat pastures, and clearly no effort had ever been made to cultivate the rocky ground on either side of the track.

She glanced down at her feet, still clad in the red espadrilles, and admitted ruefully to herself that Howard was right. She wouldn't need to mountain-climb to explore the site, but it certainly wouldn't do her white sandals much good. The espadrilles would be far more suitable footwear.

She watched him from the car for a while, as he stalked over the rocky ground and bent now and then to peer at it more closely. Then he looked up and waved her over, so she scrambled out of the car, put on her sunhat, and stumbled over to join him.

'See?' he said. 'This is one of my markers.' He pointed to a small metal peg, driven into a patch of stony soil. 'I pegged out a ten-metre square when I first identified this site fifteen years ago. Most of the markers ought to be here still: I doubt if many people stop here, and those who do wouldn't have any cause to move them. So our first job is to find them, replace any missing ones, and rope off the site—just so we know where we're looking.'

'You want me to look for pegs like this one?'

'Please.'

Half an hour later they had the small square of ground roped out. Then Howard fetched his camera and handed Belinda his clipboard, with form attached, and they began to catalogue the wild flower population.

'I don't count every flower,' he explained—to Belinda's relief! 'What I'm trying to do is to assess how air and rainwater pollution are affecting the plant population. So every five years I need to discover what types of plant are growing, and how densely. Ten years ago, for instance, that corner over there was thick with anemones. There are still plenty of flowers there today, but even at a glance I can see that the anemones are scarcer, and more robust species have gained ground.'

'So you list each species.'

'They're on the form, yes, with spaces for any new-comers at the bottom. And the form has to be completed using a scale to indicate how prevalent each one is.'

It proved to be slow and laborious work, but she didn't find it tedious. It would have been impossible not to be infected by Howard's enthusiasm, or impressed by his knowledge. He didn't just dictate the names; he took the trouble to show her each species and tell her something about it. To him this was no commonplace stretch of stony ground with a few wild flowers growing. It was a complex eco-system, maintaining a delicate balance against the ravages of man, insects and climate.

He handled each plant with an intense gentleness, his manner absorbed, his expression tender. This wasn't just a job to him, she could see. He had a real passion for the plants, and an obsessive concern for their fate in a polluted world. For all his reserved manner and contained strength, she had a growing sense of him as a deeply sensitive man.

He was too absorbed in the work to think of stopping to drink or eat, but Belinda wasn't, and after they had worked for an hour she insisted that they refresh them-selves with a drink. At one o'clock she declared a lunch break. They sat by the car, just outside the precious square of ground they were working on, eating sand-wiches and big juicy oranges, drinking mineral water, and enjoying the peace and the warmth of the day.

Once a small truck drove past, and twice Cretan women passed with donkeys in tow, but otherwise they worked on undisturbed.

It was close to six o'clock when Howard finally pronounced himself satisfied with their day's work—and still the square of land was only half catalogued. They would return the following day, he said, and Belinda, already more weary then she could have believed from a day spent in the sunshine, started on the long bumpy drive back to their hotel.

That evening the two of them ate the bland international food of the hotel restaurant. They were both too tired to talk with great animation, they drank only an ouzo apiece, and by the time supper was over Belinda felt more than ready for bed.

She apologised for wanting to turn in so early, but Howard assured her that he too was exhausted, and happy to join her.

In what sense? she wondered, as they walked side by side to the hotel lift. She had enjoyed his company during the day and over supper, and she reckoned that on the whole he'd enjoyed hers, but she couldn't really kid herself that he'd been acting like a lover towards her. On the contrary, he seemed to have taken care all day to firmly establish their relationship as boss and secretary.

Which he had, perfectly successfully, but it made things jolly difficult now. She didn't like the idea of pretending that the previous night hadn't happened, and she certainly didn't want to nudge Howard into telling her he thought it had been a mistake he didn't plan to repeat.

What she wanted was to sleep with him again, now that both of them were sober, and firmly establish *that* side of their relationship. True, she was tired, but she was still very physically conscious of him. She wasn't too tired to touch him, to kiss him, to make love with him, and what better end could there be to a glorious, if hardworking day?

She wanted him to want her, in all the ways he'd wanted her the night before—and more, because she knew him a little better now, and he her, and she felt that they were already developing a more solid base of affection and understanding.

The lift jolted to a stop at their floor, and Howard walked with her down the corridor. His room was further down than hers. She paused at her door, meaning to say 'goodnight' and before she could get the words out he said quickly, 'May I come in?'

'I was wondering if you. . .'

'Want you?' he finished for her, in a low, intense voice, 'I didn't think I'd left you in much doubt about that.'

His eyes, a deep clear grey, held hers steadily. And as she relaxed in a smile, she saw the corners crinkle, and an answering smile soften the strong lines of his face.

'You could just remind me. . .' she whispered teasingly.

'Let me do that.' He gathered her to him right there in the corridor, and claimed her lips with an arrogant confidence that left her body tingling and clamouring for more, her tiredness forgotten.

They just about managed to get the door open and closed again behind them, and after that Belinda was conscious of nothing but Howard for a very long time.

The alarm call she'd booked the night before dragged her to wakefulness next morning—and, with it, the realisation that she was alone.

Again. Had he just got up? She reached over and felt

the mattress on the other side of the bed, but she couldn't sense his warmth. She couldn't see the dent of his head in the other pillow. She couldn't remember him leaving the night before, but then she'd been so weary she had most likely fallen asleep the moment he'd finished making love to her.

He might have done the same! There was something cold-blooded about the thought of him getting up instead, dressing—well, putting back his shorts at least—and retreating down the corridor to his own room. She couldn't see any reason why he shouldn't have stayed with her, slept with her, woken up with her.

But he hadn't.

Strange man, she thought, as she eased herself out of bed and stretched herself by the window. She couldn't remember drawing the curtains the night before, but they were closed now. Had he done that too?

It seemed to her that his behaviour was odd, but then she didn't have much experience of men, so maybe she wasn't much of a judge. There had only been Paul before him. And physically what she and Paul had enjoyed hadn't been a patch on the ecstasy Howard had awoken her to, but her lovemaking with Paul had been nice in other ways. They'd always had a good laugh together, teasing and chatting before and after and even during their lovemaking.

Howard didn't tease and chat. In fact, she couldn't remember him saying a word to her after they'd come into her room.

It wasn't as if he'd been aggressive or hostile or unpleasant—not at all. But somehow their physical intimacy hadn't brought with it—yet—the mental intimacy she had so enjoyed with Paul. She knew barely a thing about Howard still. He was like a stranger to her, even though they'd enjoyed such surpassingly glorious physical experiences.

She wanted to know much, much more about him: what he thought, how he lived, his family, what made him tick. She wanted him to know more about her. After two glorious nights she felt sure they hadn't really made a mistake in going to bed together so quickly, but that didn't alter the fact that now they needed to develop the mental side of their relationship.

Still, she thought, as she crawled out of bed and under the cold shower, it's early days. We'll be together all day, and this time, instead of asking him about the Minoans, I'll get him to talk about himself.

That didn't happen over breakfast, though. Howard wasn't such a sore-headed bear that morning, but he made it clear that he was no early-morning chatterer. They ate their rolls in silence, then over their second cups of coffee he filled her in with the details of his work plans.

That day, he explained, they would finish cataloguing the site near Tsagaraki. The following day he planned to drive off alone and do some general reconnoitring, while Belinda stayed at the hotel and typed up her notes. Then they'd start work on a new site, a few miles in the opposite direction, and then would come the weekend.

They set off promptly at eight-thirty again. Now that the road and the car were more familiar, Belinda managed to drive more rapidly. And once they were clear of Heraklion, she said, 'OK, tell me about yourself.'

'What?'

'I hardly know anything about you, Howard. Tell me a little.'

'Well, I've worked at the Plant Research Unit ever since I graduated. For my PhD I studied the effects of

acid rain on wild flowers, and now I'm studying pollution effects more widely. But you know that already.'

'I don't want to know about work, I want to know
about you.'

'I don't particularly like talking about myself.'

'Most people do! Why, have you got any terrible
secrets to hide?'

'Of course not!'

'Well, then. I'll ask you questions if it's easier. How
many brothers and sisters have you got?'

'None. I'm an only child.'

'Poor you. Do you have lots of aunts and uncles and
cousins?'

'I've just got one—look, I really don't want to talk
about that kind of thing.'

'But I want to know. One cousin, you said? Male or
female? Living in Melchester, or somewhere else?'

'I think you should concentrate on the driving.'

'I am doing, but I can talk at the same time.'

'Well, if you don't mind, I'd rather not talk at the
moment.'

For a moment Belinda, chastened, fell silent. Then
she tried again.

'I'll tell you what, I'll tell you all about my family.
There's three of us: me, my elder brother Keith—he's
married now—and my younger sister Charmian. I find
it really hard to imagine what it must be like to be an
only child. Charmian's only two years younger than me,
and I can't remember a time when she wasn't around. I
always had her or Keith to play with, usually both of
them. And our house was always full of other kids, and
visiting grown-ups, and—well, it still is. It's a family
joke that between the five of us we know everybody in
Melchester.'

'Really?' Howard said in a cool voice.

'Oh, even you. I remember when Mum saw your advert in the paper I said, anyone know who he is? And Charmian had met you. You probably remember, at the Briggses' party. She said you talked to her about flowers in the kitchen. She's an inch taller than me, and her hair's longer and darker—more light brown, really, where mine's fair—but other than that people say we're very alike. They're really nice, the Briggses, aren't they? Are they good friends of yours?'

'Not especially.'

'Who are your best friends, then?'

'Most of my friends come from the University.'

'Well, they would, wouldn't they? I suppose most of Mum and Dad's friends work with one or the other of them. Dad's a solicitor, at Jones and Buckingham, and Mum teaches at Miller Road Secondary. Ted and Muriel Arnold are their best friends. Ted's a senior partner at Jones and Buckingham like Dad, and Muriel teaches French at Miller Road, so they qualify twice over. Funny how some couples fit together like that, isn't it? Rather like marrying somebody with the same birthday as you.'

'That's not so much of a coincidence.'

'Don't you think so? I do! I think it's really funny when couples share a birthday, and it's quite common, you know.'

'Once in every three hundred and sixty-five marriages, I expect.'

'Oh, much more common than that. It's something to do with astrology, that's what I think. I always like men who are Geminis like me, and Leo men, and Aquarians. What's your star sign?'

'I haven't the faintest idea.'

'When's your birthday, then?'

'August the fourteen—oh, this is ridiculous!'

'That's Leo!' she cried triumphantly. 'I knew it! You're a typical Leo man, Howard. Leo men tend to be fairly tall, and broad-shouldered, and sort of contained but forceful. And that's you absolutely, isn't it?'

'I'm not sure I'd describe myself in precisely those terms.'

'Well, I would. And I'm a typical Gemini: chatty and curious and easygoing.'

'That's certainly true.'

'All the books say that Gemini women get on really well with Leo men, so that's really good,' she said happily. 'My dad's a Sagittarian, and my mum's Libra. They're a good match too.'

'Really?'

'They're ever such a happy couple. They have rows—well, we all do—but they never sulk. It's all out there and over with in a flash. I've got such a nice family. Are your parents happy?'

'You'd have to ask them.'

'Maybe I will.' Belinda negotiated the next bend, then turned to smile at him. But his face was hard-set, she saw, and he wasn't smiling back, or even looking at her.

'Did I say something wrong?' she asked more gently.

'I told you, I don't like to talk about myself.'

'But I want to. . . But we. . .' Common sense got the better of curiosity. Head-on attacks clearly weren't going to get her anywhere. She'd have to wait for a better opportunity, then try a more subtle approach. 'Silence gets to me. Could you stand to play some music?'

'I'll try the radio if you like, but the reception won't be good up in the mountains.'

'My Walkman's on the back seat.'

He hesitated, then reached over for it and the bag of tapes she'd left next to it.

'You choose something to play,' she encouraged him.

He began to look the tapes over, turning them so that he could read the titles.

'I don't know most of these.'

'What have you got there? Oh, Alexander O'Neil! He's really good—you'll like him. Play that one.'

She half expected him to refuse, but in fact he slotted the tape into the machine and switched it on, at fairly low volume. He'd rather listen to my tapes than talk, she thought prosaically. How strange! She liked to talk about herself, and liked to hear about other people even more. But Howard didn't seem interested either in telling her anything, or in hearing her own revelations.

And perhaps he wasn't interested in hearing Alexander O'Neil, but he listened in silence, and soon Belinda was wrapped up in the rhythm of the music, the bumps and jolts of the appalling road all but forgotten.

CHAPTER FOUR

THE following day Belinda stayed at the hotel, and typed up the notes she had been making on Howard's portable computer. Howard took the Seat, and drove off. She didn't ask where he was going, and he didn't tell her.

It was a relief not to have to travel long distances in the hot and bumpy car, but on the other hand it was boring to work alone in her hotel room. She took the computer on to the balcony so that she could enjoy the sun while she worked, but that didn't make her any less lonely.

She wasn't used to being alone while she worked. At Cornwell Electronics she had done plenty of typing, but there had always been other girls just down the corridor, so that she could pause regularly and go to chat, or to deliver some memos, or to get a cup of coffee.

She treated herself to a good supply of cold drinks— and a shower at lunchtime—and in the early afternoon she set out to find somebody to talk to.

The hotel was barely a quarter full with early-season holidaymakers, and most of the surrounding hotels were still closed for the winter. The beach, the hotel foyer and the bar were all virtually deserted. But when Belinda sat down with a glass of Coke at a table outside the bar, she was invited to join a couple of middle-aged women sitting at another table.

Mrs Andrews and Mrs Wells, a widow and a divorcée, had come to Crete together to look at the Minoan ruins, and they talked interestingly not only about Knossos, the only site Belinda had heard of, but of Mallia, Phaestos, and an assortment of other, less well-known sites that they had visited, or intended to visit.

Belinda left them half an hour later with some good ideas for places to go at the weekend, and temporarily revived spirits. But her enthusiasm soon flagged once she was back at the computer.

She missed Howard, that was it. Friendly middle-aged ladies were all very well, but neither they, nor anyone else in Crete, could make up for the absence of Howard Henderson.

Maybe Howard didn't like to talk about himself, but they had still talked a great deal on the couple of days they had worked together, and she found his conversation fascinating. She was annoyed and intrigued and attracted and lustful and. . . She felt and thought so much about him that, without him to claim her attention, Crete suddenly seemed an unexpectedly dull and empty place.

What was worse, he wasn't back by the time she had all the notes transcribed, perfect down to the last dot and comma, *and* her hotel room tidied and the rest of her clothes put away. She sunbathed alone, and paddled, though she didn't plunge into the sea again. But none of these activities made up for Howard's continuing absence.

At six o'clock she retired back to her room and began to get ready for the evening. At least he was sure to want to eat when he returned! Perhaps they could explore the resort a little and find a really good restaurant, she thought, as she began to paint her fingernails and toenails a bright pink.

The dress she chose was lime-green, uncrushable

polyester, with a short skirt, side slits, and a low neckline lined with ruffles. It was fun and sexy and slightly outrageous, and by the time she had washed, dried and curled her hair, perfected her make-up and drenched herself in perfume Belinda was feeling much livelier.

She put a Madonna tape into her Walkman, leaving off her earphones so that she'd hear when Howard knocked on the door of her room, curled up on the bed with a romance to read, and was halfway through Chapter Two by the time he appeared.

'Hello, stranger!' she sang out as she opened the door to him. 'Had a busy day?'

'Yes, very,' he agreed. He was wearing khaki shorts and a white short-sleeved T-shirt. His legs and arms were already beginning to tan, and, unless it was her imagination, his hair had been bleached slightly by the sun. He was tired, she could see, and hot, but he looked satisfied and confident and very, very masculine.

'There are bottles of ouzo and water and orange juice cooling in the sink, or we can go down to the bar if you'd rather,' she told him.

'An ouzo here would be marvellous.'

'At your service, sir.' She grinned, set her hands on his shoulders and gave him a quick kiss, then nipped into the shower-room to fetch the bottles.

When she came back, Howard had subsided on to the bed.

'Strong or weak?' she asked.

'Fairly strong. Belinda, where on earth do you get your clothes from?'

'Like it? It's fun, isn't it?'

'Fun? Well. . .there's only one thing to do with a dress like that.'

'And what might that be?'

'Take it off you.'

He said this in a low, sensuous voice that stopped her in her tracks. She paused, his glass in her hand, and turned to look at him. His eyes, scanning her intently, reinforced the message, while the smile on his face took any sting of criticism out of his words.

Slowly he got up from the bed, crossed over to her, took the glass and had a sip of ouzo, then put it down again.

Belinda watched him, hypnotised by desire. He reached out a long-fingered hand and drew his forefinger in a long vertical line down the front of her dress, as if he was unzipping it. Then he caught the hemline with both hands and tugged it upwards.

She raised her arms and let him ease it over her head. They descended, naturally enough, around his neck. He caught her round the waist and drew her to him, his mouth finding hers, his hands sliding down to her buttocks and pulling her even closer so that she could feel the hard evidence of his arousal.

'And we'll take that off too,' he went on, sensuously, teasingly, tracing his fingers around the top of her bra, and then locating the catch at the back. 'That's. . .much. . .better. . .'

He punctuated his words with little kisses on the soft mounds of her breasts, and then his mouth found one rosy nipple, and he stopped talking.

Belinda squirmed with pleasure. Howard's love-making was so subtle, so expert: he knew exactly how to touch her so as to set her body alight. Each caress of his hands, each flick of his tongue, felt absolutely right. She'd never understood what her girl friends meant when they talked of aching to be with their lovers: she had enjoyed being with Paul, but he had never aroused anything approaching this urgent desire in her.

Howard's hands gently slid off the tiny scrap of lace and ribbon that was her last remaining garment. Hunger, thirst, tiredness all forgotten, she reached for the hem of his T-shirt and caressed the firm, smooth skin beneath it. He helped her pull it over his head, let his shorts follow it to the floor, then drew her over to the bed.

He sat on the edge and she straddled him, sliding down so that she was resting on his muscular thighs, and could feel the hair on them brushing against the sensitive skin of her own inner thighs. As she leaned forward to kiss him, her nipples brushed against the fair curling hair on his chest. The sensation was exquisite and agonising, like somebody lightly ticking the soles of her feet.

Howard's lips dropped little teasing kisses on the corners of her mouth, the tip of her nose, her eyelashes. His hands traced the lower contour of her breasts, then slid down the faint curve of her stomach.

She wriggled, trying to pull him sideways on to the bed, but he held her still, taunting her—taunting both of them with their longing. She brought a hand down and fumblingly tried to pull down his underpants, and he let himself fall backwards on to the bed, dragging her down on top of him.

'Let me get these off,' he grunted, surfacing to kick off his pants and sandals. Then he was as naked as she, and they were wrestling together on the broad surface of the bed, with the evening sun still flooding in through the open windows of the room.

Belinda wrapped her legs around his thigh, rubbing to and fro to try and release the intense tension inside her. The steady insistent beat of the Madonna tape was still pounding away from the Walkman she had set by the bed, and now both of them were moving in time to it. Howard's lips claimed her again, and his tongue began to fence with hers in a complex rhythmic game of hide and seek.

He moved again, withdrawing his leg, and for a moment she arched in desperate longing. Then he was positioning himself, and plunging into her, and the rhythm was drowning them both in its greedy insistence.

The pleasure seemed to flood through her in waves, mounting to a crescendo and then slowly, slowly subsiding till she was lying, damp with sweat and panting slightly, in Howard's arms.

'I need a shower,' he announced a moment later, swinging himself off the bed. 'Mind if I use yours?'

'Go ahead.' Belinda propped herself up and watched him as he strode over to the low table and retrieved his ouzo. What a beautiful body he had, strong and fit and elegant. Her eyes drank in the curve of his back, the width of his shoulders, the tapering V of fair hair on his chest and upper stomach.

He picked up her orange juice and brought it over to her. She smiled, and he smiled too, but he didn't say anything. Then he disappeared into the shower-room, and she heard the water begin to flow.

The tape ended with a defiant click, and there was no sound left but the hiss and splash of Howard showering. Belinda took a gulp of the orange juice. It tasted acidic. The evening wasn't as warm now, and she shivered as the sweat began to dry on her. Her make-up was ruined, her dress lay in a crumpled heap on the floor, and she too needed another shower.

It wasn't any of these minor irritations that set a sour edge on her happiness, though. It was Howard.

Am I so unreasonable, she asked herself, to want to hear him say 'I love you'? That's the fourth time we've made love in as many days, and he hasn't said it yet. He hasn't said anything loving to me at all. He lets me call him 'darling', but he doesn't call me 'darling' back. He just calls me Belinda.

She had been telling herself he was a little repressed: a typical reserved Englishman of the type that squirmed when people showed feelings too openly. Perhaps that was true. But if it embarrassed him to say the words out loud he could have made up for it with gestures of affection that gave out the same message.

She hadn't had any of those from him either. He acted like a casually friendly workmate, except when he was making love to her. And as soon as he'd finished he was up and off with barely a hug to spare.

It was all very well telling herself she'd change that, but she hadn't got far in changing it yet.

I'll have another go over supper tonight, she told herself.

She turned to the Walkman, and put on another tape of loud, cheerful pop music. She retrieved her dress from the floor and gave it a shake. The creases fell out, fortunately, and she would be able to put it back on after she'd showered.

The door of the shower-room opened and out came Howard, with a towel wrapped round his waist and another in his hand. He looked cool and fit, his hair still sleek and dark with water.

'Turn that row down a bit,' he said.

'It isn't a row. It's Michael Jackson, pop superstar.'

Howard, now occupied in vigorously rubbing himself

dry, didn't answer. 'I've left you a bit short of dry
towels,' he said. 'If you want to shower now I'll fetch a
couple from my room.'

'Yes, I do, please.'

He began to put on his underpants. Belinda padded,
barefoot and naked, across the floor to the shower-room.
She hesitated when she came close to him, but his
manner was so self-contained that she didn't like to stop
and beg a kiss.

How stupid! she chided herself, as she stood under the
hot jets of water. One minute we make passionate love,
and the next I'm shy of asking him for a kiss! He'd been
considerate enough, fetching her drink and noticing her
need for towels, but still she somehow felt put down.

She showered quickly, barely glancing up when
Howard came in and propped a couple of clean towels
on the side of the washbasin. She dried herself in the
shower-room, though it was damp and steamy now, and
went back into the bedroom.

Howard was fully dressed now in jeans and a white
shirt, sitting in a chair by the balcony, and drinking his
ouzo. Belinda was conscious of his eyes on her as she
reached for her dress.

'Don't put that on again,' he said. 'Wear something
else.'

'It's not crushed—it'll be all right.'

'It's too short. Too sexy.'

He smiled, and raised his glass to her, but she wasn't
in a mood to be won round. It wasn't too sexy for you a
few minutes ago, she thought belligerently, as she pulled
the dress back over her head. She brushed her hair and
redid her make-up, leaving her own drink untouched as
he poured himself a second one.

'We'll eat at the harbour again, shall we?' he asked.

'It's nearly eight now, so it's too late to go into Heraklion.'

'OK.' She glanced at her reflection in the mirror, decided she looked grumpy, and gave a big practice smile. She could see the reflection of Howard standing behind her, looking tall and fair and handsome, and she smiled again, at it. She saw his reflection smile too.

Perhaps she was being silly, getting het up over nothing. He might not say it, but hadn't he just proved in the most emphatic way that he loved her?

Howard took her hand as they made their way to the lift, so she could hardly complain about his stand-offishness. Or his being taciturn, because he took up most of the walk to the harbour in telling her about his day's work, before asking her about her day.

'Today we have lobster,' the waiter greeted them. 'Caught from the boats here this morning.'

'Then we'll have one each, shall we?'

'Wonderful!' Belinda agreed.

They sat at the terrace table they had sat at before. There was a group of fishermen on the next table, as well as another further along the terrace, and a couple of them gave Belinda long looks as she smoothed down her short dress and settled herself in her chair.

It was an awfully short dress, she thought suddenly. The fishermen's eyes were on her legs, and no wonder, because it did expose a lot of leg. And rather a lot of breast too, above the green ruffles.

How strange! She'd worn the dress a dozen times before, to parties and discos, and never thought twice about its short skirt and low neckline. She'd known it was sexy, but she'd treated that as a bit of a joke.

It didn't seem such a joke with the eyes of half a dozen swarthy men fixed on the flesh it revealed.

Belinda liked emphatic clothes that showed off her body, but she never really intended them as a come-on to men. She chose them because she felt good in them, and bother those who said that she had the most appalling dress sense! But somehow she *felt* sexy now, in a way that she simply hadn't done before. It was as if she hadn't understood before what it was to be sexually aware.

Howard had certainly taught her that. She was so intensely conscious of him, and of her desire for him. Her body still remembered every touch of his, and quivered at the thought that he'd maybe make love to her again when they returned to the hotel.

Did the fishermen sense that? she wondered. Did they guess that she and Howard had just been making love? Most likely they did, she thought with a flush of embarrassment.

She had never really thought before about how she appeared to men. They gave her lustful looks, certainly, but her manner, friendly but not particularly flirtatious, kept her from getting into too much trouble. Now she suddenly saw herself as the fishermen must see her: a pretty young blonde with a good figure, wearing a very revealing scrap of a dress, being shown off on the arm of her lover.

A bimbo, that was the word. Bubbly, sexy, available to any man with the right bank balance, without any real feelings or a thought in her head. A cartoon female, useful only for sex, thought about by men only when they wanted sex.

Was that how Howard saw her too?

She couldn't bring herself to look at him, as her mind reversed at top speed through all the scenes of their short acquaintance. Luckily he was absorbed in collecting

their wine from the waiter and pouring it, and he didn't
notice how distracted she was.

It fitted. It fitted horribly well. Howard certainly
desired her, but when she thought about it now she
couldn't find any evidence that he felt more than desire
for her. He'd acted as a reasonably thoughtful boss, as
an appreciative sexual partner: and that was all.

But she wasn't a bimbo! Surely he knew she wasn't
that sort of a girl?

And how would he know that? a sarcastic voice inside
her head whispered. Men normally found that out when
she friendlily but firmly refused their advances, but she
hadn't refused Howard's advances at all. On the contrary, she had fallen eagerly into his arms.

She had done that, of course, because of the way she
felt about him. Liking, desire, that instinctive feeling
that they were perfectly matched: love was the word that
summed it up, the word she would have used, by then,
without hesitation. He was unique to her, the only man
ever to arouse such strong desires and feelings in her.

She had hesitated to say that too clearly to him,
though, because he hadn't said the same to her. Perhaps
he hadn't realised how she felt about him; perhaps he
imagined that she acted in the same abandoned way
with every presentable man who crossed her path.

Perhaps he acted in the same way with every presentable female who crossed *his* path!

It was less than an hour since she'd been admiring his
expertise as a lover. What she hadn't thought about then
was the way in which he must have acquired that
expertise: by making love to many, many women. Not
cartoon women, not the bimbos who barely existed
outside the imagination of tabloid journalists, but real
flesh-and-blood women. Women who desired him, who

most likely believed they were falling in love with him. Women who hurt, hurt badly, when they realised that he hadn't fallen in love with them.

Women like her. Well, not exactly like her, because every person was unique, after all, but maybe not all that different from her.

Howard was thirty-one. She couldn't have been the first woman to admire his powerful good looks, to appraise his career prospects, to enjoy his conversation, and to decide she'd like him for herself. He was special to her—but just how special was she to him?

She wasn't special enough for him to want to tell her all about himself.

This realisation hit her with the force of a ten-ton truck. That was what lovers did, after all. They wanted to know all about their loved one, and to tell him or her all about themselves. They shared ideas and secrets and confidences. Howard didn't.

She had already noticed this, of course, but she had been telling herself that Howard didn't want to talk about himself because of his natural reserve. Maybe it wasn't that at all, though. Maybe he simply didn't think of her as somebody he wanted to be close to, in any but a physical sense.

That idea appalled her.

How blithe, how naïve she had been! She was pretty, Howard fancied her, she was falling in love with Howard—therefore he was falling in love with her? If she had been listening to Charmian, or to any of her girl friends, describing an affair like the one she and Howard had started, she would have been quick enough to warn them that they were building their castles—not even on air, but on the most lethal of vacuums.

She wanted to be wrong. She wanted it desperately.

But she could see now that she'd been taking a dangerous amount for granted.

'Aren't you drinking?' Howard asked casually.

'Oh. Yes.' Belinda grabbed her glass. What a good idea! Her solid self-confidence didn't normally need the artificial boost of alcohol, but right now it had turned into a mirage. She felt frighteningly transparent and vulnerable, and needed anything, even a swig of wine, that would help to veil over her panic.

'So what did these women tell you?' Howard asked.

'These—these women?' she echoed.

'The ones you were talking to this afternoon.'

'Oh—them.'

Must talk naturally. Mustn't let him see what you're thinking. With a tremendous effort of will, Belinda pushed her fears to the back of her mind, and tried to recall some of what Mrs Andrews and Mrs Wells had told her about Ancient Crete.

She chattered, first desperately, then a little more easily, about the ruins they had advised her to visit. Howard responded quite naturally, with questions and short comments of his own. But she couldn't help judging each of his responses now, and it soon became clear to her that he wasn't really interested in what she was saying.

That unnerved her even more. She never normally considered whether she might be boring people. She chattered away cheerfully and took it for granted that they enjoyed her company and conversation. But perhaps Howard didn't? Perhaps he really was bored, and was only showing the polite interest that any man would need to show when he was obliged to take his secretary out to dinner?

Her conversation faltered, and when the waiter brought bread and Greek salad she lapsed into silence.

Their silence continued until their coffee came. The fishermen had paid their bill and left the taverna, and apart from the waiter lingering in the doorway to the kitchen they were the only people left.

'You're very quiet tonight,' Howard said suddenly.

'Am I? It's the after-effect of all that bang-banging on the typewriter, I expect.' Belinda forced a smile.

'I'm sorry—I'm not being much company either. I've been wrapped up thinking about the plants.'

'Have you come to any conclusions yet, or is it too early for that?'

'I can see an overall trend, but then that's pretty much what I expected. The effect of pollution isn't as dramatic here as it is in Northern Europe, but some of the more delicate species have been affected.'

'Which ones?' She did her best to show an interest, and soon Howard was talking earnestly about his work.

That subject certainly fascinates him, she thought bitterly, as she smiled and nodded at his explanations and statistics. But it's nothing to do with me, is it? I'm just the dumb secretary. He's only telling me about it because there's nobody else who's interested.

And though she was interested, in her way, she couldn't bring all her attention to bear on the problems of industrial pollution. What she wanted to know about was Howard Henderson; what he really thought and felt, what made him tick. And she seemed further than ever from finding out.

'Let's go,' Howard said, when their coffee cups had been cleared away. 'It's been a long day.'

'You're tired.'

'Not too tired to make love to you again when we get back.'

He whispered this as they were passing from the bay to the track that led inland, and squeezed her hand. But Belinda couldn't bring herself to meet his look, or smile in response to his smile. Yes, you want that; but is that all you want? she couldn't help asking herself.

'Have you had a lot of girlfriends?'

'Girlfriends?' Howard walked on a while, and she thought for a moment that he wasn't going to answer her. Then he said casually, 'About the usual number, I suppose.'

'And what is the usual number?'

'I don't know. I've never gone in for keeping count.'

'Two or three? A dozen? Hundreds?'

'What is this, an inquisition? Not hundreds, of course not. I'd have no time for work if I did that, would I?'

'But quite a lot. Enough for you to lose count.'

Howard stopped in his tracks, and turned to confront her. 'I'm thirty-one, Belinda. You weren't expecting to be the first, were you?'

'No. But I hadn't really thought about being the fifty-first, either.'

'You're not—nothing like. Look, if you really want to know, I broke up a few months ago with a woman I'd been seeing for nearly five years. And there's nobody else back in England now, so you've nothing to worry about.'

'What was her name?'

'Deirdre—Deirdre Shannon. But it doesn't matter.'

'What doesn't matter? Her name, or you breaking up with her after five years?'

'None of it matters all that much. I'm not heartbroken, if that's what you're wondering. I'm not pining for her.'

'Are you sorry? Was it you who wanted to split up, or her?'

'She did. She met somebody else and married him. But I said it doesn't matter. Forget it, Belinda.'

'But it *does* matter. You matter to me. And what you feel, what you do, what you used to do, who you did it with, all that matters to me.'

'Well, now you know.'

'Not much I don't. What was she like, this Deirdre?'

'All right. Look, it's getting cold. Let's get back to the hotel.'

'You really don't think I ought to be interested in all this, do you?'

'I can tell you're interested, but I don't particularly want to talk about it. Come on, Belinda.'

'Was she like me?'

'No, nothing like you.' Howard took her hand and almost pulled her along the path to the hotel.

'Did she ask you lots of personal questions?'

'No.'

'She didn't ask you questions? You went on seeing her for *five years*, and she didn't want to know all about you?'

'Not everybody does.' Howard stopped again. 'If you want the truth, Belinda,' he said in an exasperated tone, 'that was one of the things I liked about her. She never pushed and pried the way you do. You're great in bed, but I don't like being worried at, and I wish you'd drop it. Now come on.'

'Great in bed? So I'm great in bed, am I?'

'Don't snarl like that. It's a compliment, for heaven's sake. Now, come on.'

'It's not a compliment!'

Howard stared at her, impatience and bewilderment mingled in his expression.

'How many boyfriends do you think I've had, Howard?' Belinda asked, in a low voice. 'How many lovers? Go on, guess. Do you think you're the fifty-first? Or the hundred and fifty-first?'

'I don't know, and frankly I don't care. I don't want you messing with other men while you're seeing me, but as for what you did before you met me, that's none of my business.'

'It *is* your business. You're my lover, and that makes it your business! So let me tell you, Howard Henderson. You're the second. One—two. The second.'

There was a moment's awful silence. Then Howard stepped a pace back, murmuring half under his breath. 'Oh, for God's sake!'

Belinda gulped. 'No, that's not quite right,' she said in an unsteady voice. 'I'd better change that. It's not that you are the second. You *were* the second. I guess you call this learning the hard way.'

She took a step away from him, and then another step. Then, as he didn't move, she began to walk more quickly—almost running, as well as she could in her high-heeled sandals. She could see the solid block of the hotel, black against the night sky, in front of her. She didn't turn round, didn't listen out for Howard's footsteps, didn't stop until she reached the cold enveloping security of its foyer. Then she paused only to collect her key, hurried to the stairs without waiting for the lift, and a moment later, shaking, she was turning the key in the lock of her room.

The bed was still rumpled where she and Howard had made love earlier. There was a faint sweet smell in the air, and on the floor were tossed, in a pile, the damp towels in which they had wrapped themselves. Belinda stood there for a moment, barely taking all of this in. Then she threw herself on to the bed, and began to cry.

CHAPTER FIVE

GETTING up next morning, and going down to breakfast, were among the hardest things Belinda had ever done. If only it had been Saturday! But it was Friday, and she and Howard were supposed to go and find the second of his wild flower sites.

In the darkest hours of the night she had thought of getting the next plane back to England, but common sense had soon prevailed. She had more pride than to give up the job simply because she'd made a fool of herself, and she knew that Howard's research budget wouldn't stretch to flying a replacement secretary out from England. No, she would carry on as best she could, and hope he would never realise quite how much he had hurt her.

She dressed in her usual bright clothes, not least because she didn't have anything more drab with her! A blue and white sailor-style top, worn with very short blue shorts, went well with the red espadrilles, and she livened the outfit up still more with a mass of coloured bangles and a wide red leather belt. Careful attention to her make-up helped to minimise the dark circles under her eyes, and bright blue eyeshadow drew attention away from them.

Howard was already in the hotel dining-room when she arrived, and resisting the temptation to choose a different table, Belinda sat down opposite him with as cheery a 'Good morning' as she could manage.

'Morning,' he responded. His manner was subdued but pleasant. 'Coffee?'

'Yes, please.'

'We're going east this morning,' he told her. 'I brought down the map, and I'll show you the route now, if that's OK with you. The site isn't in the mountains this time; it's quite close to the sea, and you'll find the roads are much better.'

'Thank goodness!'

He spread his map across the table, and they discussed the site and what he hoped to find there for the rest of the meal.

He left Belinda to drink her second cup of coffee alone, telling her he'd see her at the car. 'I'll be there,' she assured him with a smile.

When he had left the room her shoulders slumped slightly, but she noticed a couple sitting on a nearby table giving her a curious glance, so she livened up again, and drank the coffee quickly.

It hadn't been so very, very bad. He had been making obvious efforts to be pleasant to her: no criticisms of her clothes, her shoes or her jewellery at all! He hadn't brought up their argument, thank heavens, and she guessed that he wouldn't, now. She'd get through the day somehow, and then would come the weekend when she wouldn't have to see so much of him, and the following week would surely be easier still.

She nipped back to her room to fetch her Walkman, and arrived at the car, keys jingling, just five minutes late.

The road east was indeed good. The sky was just a little overcast, but it was pleasant weather for driving, and since neither of them were in a mood to talk Howard played one of Belinda's tapes, rather loud. He turned it off when they reached the turning off the main road, and soon they were approaching the site, on a stretch of rocky ground within sight of the sea.

'It's always rocky ground you choose,' Belinda grumbled—but in a deliberately cheerful voice—as she stumbled around looking for the half-hidden markers.

'It has to be. On Crete every scrap of fertile land's farmed, and I need to study virgin soil for this research. I've tried to choose a cross-section of sites, lowland and higher land, well watered and dry, but inevitably they're all the kind of rocky, infertile ground that won't do for olives or bananas.'

'Bananas? I haven't seen those.'

'Oh, yes, you have.' He smiled, and his eyes looked for hers, though she didn't meet his gaze. 'We must have passed at least a dozen of the hothouses this morning.'

'Those big plastic things, you mean?' She had indeed noticed the wooden frameworks covered in plastic sheeting, but she had been too absorbed in appearing happy to think of asking what grew in them.

'That's right. Those cover the banana groves.'

'I could just eat a nice ripe sweet banana now.'

'There are a couple in the hamper. I'll get you one.'

'There's no——' she began, but he had already set off to the car.

And, irresistibly, her eyes followed him.

Oh, he was gorgeous. He might be heartless, self-contained, unreasonably casual about sex, but he was still the most beautiful man she'd ever seen. He's bad news, she told herself firmly, but her body, melting inside as she watched his easy strides across the rough ground, didn't agree with her.

As she watched he raised the tailgate of the Seat,

rummaged in the hamper, then glanced over at her and waved two small bananas in triumph.

Guilty at having been caught watching him, Belinda hastily transferred her gaze to the stony soil. But she didn't see any markers in the next few minutes, not least because she was acutely conscious of him striding back towards her.

'This one's for you.'

She reached out a hand and took it, being careful not to touch him. Go away, she thought desperately, but he didn't. He stood there, a bare pace away from her, and began to peel the skin off his own banana.

They ate them in silence, standing side by side. 'I'll put the skins in the rubbish bag,' Howard said.

'I'll do that.' It was no good standing there watching him—she wanted to be busy. And when she returned from the car Howard himself was busy, roping off the square of bumpy ground.

They worked steadily until lunchtime. The sky slowly cleared, and the sun began to beat down strongly on them. The air was soft with the buzzing of bees among the gorse bushes and the fragile anemones. Belinda had to concentrate to follow all the complex botanical names, and there wasn't space in her mind to hold her pain there all the time.

She and Howard found some big smooth rocks, just beyond the site, to sit on while they ate their lunch. The hamper held feta cheese and tomato sandwiches, plastic pots of thick creamy yogurt wrapped in damp cloths to keep them cool, more bananas, and cans of fizzy lemonade. It was an enjoyable meal, in glorious surroundings, and if it was disturbing to be aware of Howard's body close to hers, his lightly bronzed skin—he was stripped to the waist—the neat movements of his long hands, at least she could try to persuade herself that there was simple pleasure in his company mixed in with her unhappiness.

As soon as she'd finished eating she busied herself clearing their rubbish back into the empty hamper.

'I'll just put this in the car,' she said.

'There's no hurry. We did well this morning, so we can afford a reasonable break now. Sit down again.'

Belinda hesitated, but she really hadn't any option but to obey him. She sat on a rock about three feet away from him, and stared out to sea.

'Belinda,' he said in a deep, gentle voice, 'I can see how it must have looked to you last night, and——'

'I don't want to talk about it,' she interrupted quickly. 'Please. Let's forget it.'

'How can we, when we've got to go on working together?' Howard retorted. 'Let me say what I meant to say. I didn't take it for granted we were going to be lovers, honestly. I've brought female assistants on field trips before, lots of times, and never become involved with them. It's just that I found you so damn irresistible, and you seemed more than willing, and. . .'

'And we got carried away,' Belinda finished for him. 'All right, it was as much my fault as yours. I'm not going to hold a grudge against you for the rest of the trip, but I'd rather not talk about it any more.'

'But you seem to want to act as if it never happened!'

'What else is there to do?'

'We could carry on as we were.'

Belinda was too astonished to remember her resolution not to look at him. And when she spun round, it was to meet his eyes, gazing levelly at her from under his heavy brows, to see the half-smile that lifted the corners of his lips.

A flash-fire of sexual hunger zipped through her, but only to be followed by a mounting tide of annoyance, as he reached forward to trap her hands in his, and continued in a softly insistent voice, 'It's not as if we really quarrelled about anything, is it? I know you felt I'd taken it for granted, and I've said I'm sorry, but it wasn't like that really. And you're still you, and I'm still me, and I can't see why we shouldn't go on enjoying each other as much as we have been doing.'

Couldn't he? The arrogant, self-satisfied, heartless man!

All right, she grudgingly conceded to herself, maybe he really couldn't.

'So you reckon we spend a month sleeping together, then shake hands and say goodbye when we get back to England?'

'It doesn't have to be like that. We'll both be going back to Melchester. There's no reason why we shouldn't carry on seeing each other for as long as we both want to.'

Her eyes lowered: she didn't dare let him see how tempted she was. And he took advantage of that to move closer, claiming half her rock, and wrapping his arms around her.

Oh, no! She set two small palms on his bare warm chest, and pushed him firmly away. 'I can think of a reason,' she said in a low but steady voice.

'What's that?'

'You don't love me.'

'Oh, for heaven's sake!' Howard loosed her abruptly, stood up, and took a couple of paces towards the shoreline. He stood there for a moment, staring out to sea. Then he turned back, before she remembered to look away from him, and said quietly, reasonably.

'What's love got to do with it? You don't love me either, not in any real sense. We barely know each other.'

'But I do want to get to know you, Howard, and you don't seem to want me to. And I don't think you want to get to know me at all.'

A faint, faint frown lowered his brows almost imperceptibly. He kept his eyes on her, and she looked steadily back. This was the core of it, and he had to understand.

He stood there, staring at her, for some time. Then slowly he moved, towards her. He sat down again by her side.

'Belinda,' he said. 'Look. You're pretty and lively and fun to be with, and I've enjoyed your company in and out of bed for the last few days. But when it comes down to it we hardly have anything in common. We don't think in the same way, we don't have the same interests and tastes. I don't want to make out I'm going to fall in love with you and marry you and it'll end happily ever after, because that wouldn't be honest. I'm not interested in falling in love and getting married, anyway. All that's not for me. There hasn't been a woman in my life for the past few months, and I'd like to change that, sure. I like to have somebody to relax with and talk to and make love with. If you want that, then fine. But I don't like to be probed and questioned and psychoanalysed. I don't want to do that to you, and I don't want you doing it to me. And I don't want you imagining that this is going to lead us to the altar, because I'll warn you now, that's not what I'm offering.'

'So you're just offering me a casual affair.'

'It needn't be all that casual. We'll be seeing plenty of each other for the next few weeks. And there won't be anyone else in my life, either here or when we get back to England, I promise. That much commitment you can certainly have from me.'

'A commitment to provide each other with fun and sex.'

'That's not exactly how I'd have put it.'

'But it's what you mean.'

He didn't answer. Belinda sat there for a moment, twisting the bangles on her wrist round and round. Then she said in a low voice, 'No. I'm sorry, but it wouldn't work.'

'It's worked fine up till now.' Howard reached out his hand and set it on her bare knee. She stared down at it. She wanted to push it away, but she hadn't put the impulse into effect before his other hand descended on her shoulder.

He drew her round to confront her, not roughly, but with an innate strength that she couldn't have resisted. His mouth found hers. His easy expert confidence had gone, but in its place was a steady determination that had an even more devastating effort on her. His hard mouth, the tongue that forced her lips apart, the hands that claimed her body, all delivered the unmistakable message that this man, this strong, masterful man, meant to be her man.

And she ached to be his woman. She could feel the current of pleasure building up in her. They were completely alone; he could have made love to her right there, and it would have been glorious.

Glorious—but wrong. A six-lane highway to heartache, if ever there was one. If she'd cared less about him she might have given in. But. . .

She wasn't a cuddly toy, to be played with and tossed aside. She wasn't the sort of person who could decide whether to fall in love, as Howard quaintly put it.

Emotions didn't work like that, and hers were already dangerously involved.

As soon as the pressure of his mouth eased, she took advantage of it to wrench her head to one side. 'No,' she panted. 'Please, Howard—no!'

'You do want me, I know you do.'

'Not like that I don't. Come on, let's get back to work.'

She struggled free of his embrace, and moved rapidly back to the wild flower site. At first Howard didn't follow her. She picked up her notepad and pretended to check through her notes for the morning. And out of the corner of her eye she could see him standing up, his graceful body suddenly heavy in its movements, and walking slowly towards her.

Howard clearly wasn't going to let his desires get in the way of his research, and their afternoon's work went smoothly. There were no awkward moments until Belinda drew up again in the hotel car park that evening.

And hesitated. The weekend stretched ahead of them. She had some more typing-up to do on Saturday morning, and presumably Howard had some work plans too, but there would be plenty of free hours to be filled. And there was supper that evening, and breakfast the next day, and lunch. . . Were they going to spend all that time together?

Were they going to eat together, swim together, sightsee together? She didn't want to let him take that for granted. If she carried on seeing so much of him, she'd really only have herself to blame if he renewed his advances—and she wasn't at all certain that she'd be able to carry on saying no to them.

But the alternative didn't hold much appeal. Eating

More Good News For Subscribers Only!

When you join the Harlequin Reader Service®, you'll receive 6 heart-warming romance novels each month delivered to your home. You'll also get additional free gifts from time to time, as well as our subscribers-only newsletter! It's your privileged look at upcoming books and profiles of our most popular authors!

If offer card is missing, write to:
Harlequin Reader Service, 3010 Walden Avenue, P.O. Box 1867, Buffalo, NY 14269-1867

breakfast alone, on opposite sides of the hotel restaurant? Going out to supper alone? Swimming and sunbathing alone? That certainly wasn't her idea of a great weekend.

She still hadn't decided what to suggest, or which suggestions of Howard's she might agree with, when they reached the reception desk. And that solved her first problem for her, for there was Mrs Andrews, one of the women she had been talking to the previous day, asking about calls to England. Belinda said hello to her while Howard was waiting to retrieve their room keys, and a little prompting persuaded the older woman to suggest that she eat with her and Mrs Wells that evening.

'And your friend. . .?' Mrs Andrews asked, sending a very interested glance over Belinda's shoulder towards Howard.

'Oh, forgive me for not introducing you. Dr Henderson, my boss; Mrs Andrews. I'm sure Dr Henderson's seen more than enough of me already today, so he won't mind in the least if I desert him over supper for once.'

Howard smiled and shook Mrs Andrews's hand, but there was a stiffness about his small talk, and Belinda sensed that he wasn't very happy about her plans. Too bad, she thought mutinously. He's the one who says that we have nothing in common. He can go off and indulge some of those interests I don't share, while I have a good gossip with some people who *are* happy to talk to me!

She took the two older women down to the taverna by the harbourside. How silly she'd been, imagining that it was her and Howard's special place. Bosses and secretaries didn't have special places. Only lovers did that, and Howard didn't love her.

It unnerved her a little to think that he might decide

to go there too. But he didn't appear, and she did her best to suppress her low spirits, and to talk animatedly to the two women.

Howard was in the hotel dining-room, alone, when Belinda went down to breakfast the next morning. But she didn't sit with him. There was a woman sitting on her own on the far side of the room, so Belinda joined her, and enjoyed an interesting chat about her new acquaintance's life as a librarian in London.

After Howard had eaten he came over to their table.

'Oh, hello,' Belinda said, rather unconvincingly.

'I just wondered—were you planning to use the car today?'

'I hadn't really thought. Did you. . .?'

'Then would it be all right with you if I take it today, and leave it to you tomorrow?'

All right! Two days without him!

'Oh—er—yes, of course.' She fished the keys out of her bag, and watched him go off with them.

'What a dishy bloke,' the librarian remarked. 'Is he your. . .?'

'He's my boss, and, I warn you, he eats women alive!'

After breakfast she took the portable computer out on to the balcony once more, and typed up her notes. She worked doggedly and fast, trying not to brood too much. By eleven o'clock she was finished, and went down to the bar and beach. There were a smattering of holiday-makers around, but Mrs Andrews and Mrs Wells had left that morning, so had the librarian, and Howard was—not surprisingly—nowhere to be seen.

Belinda sunbathed till lunchtime. A German holiday-maker came up and invited her to have a drink with him, and she snapped at him so sharply that he snapped back that he hadn't meant to be rude, and made her feel quite guilty. She even thought of calling after him and accepting the drink after all, but she wasn't too happy about drinking with strange men, so she reluctantly let him go away unappeased.

She lunched alone. And that was more than she could stand of being on her own in the hotel, so she asked at reception about buses into Heraklion, and was told that one went hourly from a stop on the main road.

She took the next one, and spent an interesting—if solitary—afternoon wandering around the shops and museums of the island's main town. She bought a book on the Minoan antiquities, partly for her own interest, and partly because she knew her mother would enjoy reading it when she got back to England; a heap of postcards to send to her family and friends; and a pretty beaten-silver ring in a small shop in a side-street.

The postcards gave her something to do once she was back at the hotel, had showered and changed—into an uncharacteristically subdued pale blue T-shirt dress— and gone down to the bar. She'd have preferred to chat to somebody, but there weren't any single women or couples in the bar, just the German tourist who had tried to pick her up earlier, and she didn't feel she could chat to him.

It wasn't as bad sitting alone at a table writing out postcards as it would have been simply staring into space. But this was only six o'clock on Saturday evening! She'd still got to face the prospect of eating supper alone, going to bed alone, and spending all the next day alone.

How *could* there be so few tourists on the island? All right, the season hadn't started yet, but she'd taken it for granted that Crete would be full of friendly English-speaking people. Fat chance. She couldn't see a single woman, a single couple even, whom she might go and chat to. And even if she did find a friend in the resort, in a day or two she and Howard would be moving on, and leaving them behind.

Maybe she shouldn't have been quite so off-putting towards him?

She was determined not to go to bed with him again, but she did have to work with him, and would it be so very different if she also socialised with him, in a friendly, platonic way? She could do her best to dress and act not at all provocatively, so that he wouldn't get the wrong impression.

If he comes back in the next half-hour, she decided, I'll ask him if we can have supper together.

She kept glancing at the door to the bar, but there was no sign of him. She ordered a second orange juice, and picked up another card.

'Good lord, how many postcards are you planning to send?'

It *was* Howard. Belinda's smile beamed out automatically, and lingered for a long instant before she remembered to tone it down.

'I won't be sending all these,' she parried. 'Only a couple of dozen. The rest are for me to keep.'

'A couple of dozen! Who on earth do you send them to?'

'Well, there's Mum and Dad and Charmian, and then there's Keith and Sally—that's my brother and his wife—and Grandad and Grandma Barford, and Granny Smith, my mother's mother, and a couple of aunts and uncles. Seven, actually: my mother has two brothers and two sisters, and my dad has three brothers. We're a big family. And lots of my cousins have left home, so I need separate cards for them. Then there are the girls at

Cornwell Electronics where I used to work, and a few people I still see from the secretarial college, and my friend Pat who I play tennis with, and Julie and Fran. . .'

'I get the picture,' Howard said. 'Like another drink to sustain you through the marathon?'

'I won't do them all tonight. And actually I've had two orange juices already.'

'Have a gin and tonic this time, then.' He didn't wait for a reply, but strode over to the bar.

Belinda watched him—as usual. He'd evidently been back for long enough to have showered and changed, though into nothing fancy—just the usual jeans and a grey short-sleeved T-shirt imprinted with a CND slogan. She doubted if he'd have spent his day sunbathing, but he was just as deeply tanned as she was—if not more so, curse him! He looked relaxed and cheerful. Where had he been? Would he bite her head off if she asked him?

She couldn't ask him just then, though, because the German tourist said something to him, and the two men rapidly fell into conversation. Howard crossed to her table to give her the drink, but returned immediately to the bar to continue talking to the German. Belinda wrote several more postcards, glancing up at him every now and then, and trying not to feel resentful because he wasn't with her.

Would he go and eat with the German? It would serve her right, she supposed, after going off to eat with Mrs Andrews and Mrs Wells the night before. If he does, though, I'll scream, she thought.

Their conversation seemed remarkably animated. What were they talking about? Did the German tourist know more about botany than she did? Was Howard having a much more interesting conversation with him than he had had with her? Maybe he's right, she thought ruefully: perhaps we really don't have much in common. Maybe I've been boring him silly every evening this week, and he's relieved to have somebody more like himself to talk to at last.

She looked down and discovered that she'd absent-mindedly scrawled all over the back of a postcard of a Minoan snake-goddess. She didn't like to risk catching Howard's attention by tearing it up, so she shoved it to the bottom of the pile and concentrated on trying to think of something to write to Pat.

'Dear Pat, having a lovely time on Crete. The sun's shining and I'm getting a super tan.' Gosh, that *was* boring! Was she really a deeply boring person? She'd never thought it before—she'd always believed she had a bubbly personality that other people warmed to. But Howard Henderson didn't warm to it. He only went for her short skirt and low neckline.

'We've found forty-seven species of flowering plants,' she wrote on. 'Botany's fascinating—think I'll take it up as a hobby! Love, Lindy.'

'Belinda, did you want to join us to eat?' said Howard's voice.

'Oh! Er—well. . .yes, please.'

'This is Gunther; he's from Bonn. He's a maths lecturer at the University there, and we've been having a very interesting conversation about university politics.'

'How fascinating.' She held out her hand and tried to look serious and interested—and as if she didn't recall her briefly embarrassing encounter with Gunther earlier in the day. 'Are you in Crete for long, Gunther?'

'For three weeks, to look at the antiquities.'

'Oh? Where have you been so far?'

The three of them walked down the main street, and settled down to eat in a rather brightly lit restaurant not far from the hotel. Belinda and Gunther continued to talk about the Minoan ruins. It rather pleased Belinda that she was able to hold her own in the conversation, thanks to Mrs Andrews and Mrs Wells, the Heraklion Museum, and the guidebook she'd been reading while she waited for the bus home. You see, Howard Henderson, she couldn't help thinking, my head isn't full of cotton wool after all! I may not be a brilliant botanist, but I do have *some* interests!

Later the conversation moved on to West German politics, and she knew enough to contribute a few remarks, thanks to Graham who always made her listen to the hour-long early evening television news. They talked about sport, and she discovered that Howard played tennis—and he discovered that her game was good enough to get her into Melchester Tennis Club's first team. They talked about photography, and she mentioned some of the tips she had learned from Paul, her one-time boyfriend and a keen amateur photographer.

So much for us having nothing in common, Howard Henderson! she thought to herself. Howard hadn't talked nearly as seriously when she and he were alone together, but Gunther's presence encouraged them to keep to heavier topics, and it was pleasing to know that she wasn't out of her depth. Surely she was making it clear to Howard that though she might look pretty and empty-headed she was no baby doll, but a solicitor's daughter with a good education and plenty of interests.

The conversation was animated enough to keep them lingering in the taverna till after midnight, and Belinda was feeling tired as they made their way back along the darkened road to the hotel. The pavement was narrow, and she and Gunther walked side by side, with Howard just behind them.

'What do you plan to do tomorrow, Gunther?' she asked.

'I visit more ruins. Tomorrow I think at Tylissos, up in the mountains, and perhaps one or two other small sites to the west of Heraklion.'

'I haven't heard of Tylissos. Is that as good as Knossos?'

'Oh, no! I've not seen it yet, but it will not be like Knossos: it is a much smaller site with less to view. You have seen Knossos, of course?'

'Not yet. I'd thought of going there tomorrow.'

'That's good. I would say, come to see Tylissos with me, but if you have not seen Knossos that will be much better. And you, Howard?' Gunther continued, glancing backwards. 'Are you looking forward to seeing Knossos too?'

'Actually I've already been there, on a previous trip to Crete. I'd be happy to see it again if Belinda wants company, but if she'd prefer to go alone then I'd rather like to join you. If you'll let me.'

'I'd be delighted,' Gunther said enthusiastically.

'Is that OK with you, Belinda?'

'Of course,' Belinda agreed, with what she hoped was a convincing air of indifference.

Howard was nowhere to be seen when she came down for breakfast the next morning, but Gunther was in the dining-room, so she joined him. He told her a little more about what she would see at Knossos, and made some suggestions for the rest of her day. He seemed to take it for granted that she was set on seeing Knossos, and she didn't like to tell him that she'd much have preferred to go with him and Howard. Anyway, she told herself, it would be wiser not to see Howard *too* much, and if she spent the day alone she'd be able to eat supper with him.

'When you've seen the palace, drive on to Arkhanes,' Gunther told her. 'It's on the Knossos road, and a nice place to have lunch. There are several Minoan sites there. They're not freely open to the public, but you can see quite a lot through the fence, or maybe you could ask at the taverna if the official guide is available. Then you can take this loop of road here, to Vathipetro, and look at the villa site there.'

'There's so much to see!'

'That's the good thing about Crete; there are sites to see everywhere. And churches: you like Byzantine churches with frescoes?'

'I like to see everything, and I want a long day out: unless it brightens up, it's too overcast for me to come back early to sunbathe.'

'Then ask the guide, and perhaps he will unlock the church at Arkhanes for you. It has some very good fourteenth-century frescoes.'

'Thanks, Gunther.'

'Have a good day.'

She *would* have a good day, Belinda told herself firmly as she started the car, even if it did have to be a solitary one. She could play her tapes as loudly as she liked with nobody to complain! She could sing along with them if she wanted to. She could stop whenever she fancied, to get an ice-cream or a Coke, or simply to look at the view. Being alone was fun.

The road to Knossos was familiar to her now, and she

found her way to the archaeological site without diffi-
culty. She found it fascinating, though rather bewilder-
ing. Her quick mugging-up of Minoan history really
didn't serve to give her much idea what the maze of
buildings would have looked like when they were com-
plete, or what each one was, but she looked all around
the site, climbing up and down the restored staircases,
admiring the bright colours of the frescoes—modern
copies of the originals she'd seen in the museum at
Heraklion—and staring in amazement at vast jars, taller
than her, in which oil and grain had been stored
thousands of years earlier.

She took a lot of photographs to show her family when
she got home, and had a long and interesting conversation with an English family of tourists when she treated
herself to a lemonade in the café opposite. Then she
returned to the Seat and unfolded her map.

The road looked to be good as far as Arkhanes, but
some of the loop Gunther had suggested, she realised
with a sinking heart, was unpaved track of the kind she
was only too familiar with. Oh, well, she'd carry on and
see where the day took her.

It took her first to a pleasant taverna in the large
village of Arkhanes, where she enjoyed *souvlaki*—chunks
of lamb, skewered with peppers and onion—and the
ubiquitous Greek salad for lunch. She asked at the
taverna about the Minoan sites that Gunther had told
her about, and after a lengthy wait she was introduced
to the guide, who unlocked the gates for her, and
provided her with the key to the frescoed church.

She was conscious that her expertise didn't really
justify this personal attention, but it was enjoyable
having somebody to show her the special features of the

sites. These quiet locations had far less to show than Knossos, but they seemed to her more atmospheric.

After summoning the guide she had to look at everything and linger for a reasonable length of time, even when she privately felt that the jumbles of stones weren't all that interesting. All the pots, frescoes and other movable items discovered had been shipped off to the Heraklion Museum. The guide's English was rudimentary, and her attempts to chat to him soon dwindled away, but she smiled a great deal to make up.

It was late afternoon by the time she was ready to leave the village. Should she go on to Vathipetro, or should she go straight back? It was still overcast, so there was no point in getting back early to sunbathe.

I'll do everything Gunther suggested, she decided. Then I'll have lots to tell Howard about over supper. Anyway, I'm getting good at driving over dirt tracks! So she set off on the road southwards.

Once in the car she wound down the windows to let plenty of air rush through, and turned on a tape of Wet Wet Wet, one of her favourite groups. This is real rural Crete, she thought happily to herself. I haven't stayed on the beaches like so many holidaymakers do: I'll have seen a cross-section of the whole island before I go home. The inland villages, with their black-dressed women, their donkeys and goats, made few concessions to tourism, and she guessed that the scene in front of her would have looked much the same fifty or a hundred years back in time.

Bump—bump—bang! The car lurched, and she slammed on the brakes.

It was, of course, a puncture. And wouldn't Howard laugh? Because there wasn't a soul in sight, so she really would have to change the wheel herself.

CHAPTER SIX

CHANGING a wheel on a Cretan dirt track wasn't quite the same as being shown how to do it in a car maintenance class, but Belinda managed to puzzle it out with the help of the car manual, and twenty minutes later she was sitting on the verge drinking a can of Coke and admiring her completed handiwork.

The effort—and the worry—had tired her, and by now she really didn't feel like looking at yet more ruins. She carried on to Vathipetro anyway, though, because she guessed from a look at her—not always reliable— map that it was by now the fastest way back to Heraklion.

She hoped that there would be a garage in Vathipetro or in one of the other villages she passed through, but they were all too tiny to stretch to one. So she drove on, still playing her music loud and wondering if Howard would be a tiny bit impressed when she modestly described how she had coped with the crisis.

It wasn't fair, wasn't fair at all, when another crisis hit her. Another puncture—and on a decent stretch of metalled road at that!—though the damage to the tyre had probably been done on the rocky stretch, she guessed, as she veered to a halt and gazed at the sullen pancake shape of the offside front wheel.

How far to the next village? Miles! She knew that from a glance at the surrounding countryside. Near the villages the lower slopes were all cultivated, and goats and sheep grazed on the higher ones, but here there was no sign of farming activity. She couldn't remember passing a reasonable-sized village in the previous few kilometres, so she locked up the car, took her sunhat, stowed her handbag and her last remaining can of Coke in her beachbag and slung it over her shoulder, and set off to walk.

Walking in Crete might be a pleasure when you chose to do it, but it wasn't a pleasure when you had to, and didn't know how far you would have to walk either. It took her a good half-hour to reach a tiny village. Then it took almost as long to discover a café which boasted a public telephone, and to explain to the elderly lady proprietor that she needed to call a garage. Even then she wasn't sure that the woman had understood, and she waited with increasing nervousness for the forty-five minutes that the breakdown truck took to arrive.

It was late now. But she still had to lead the garage man to her abandoned car; watch him change the wheel with a speed and efficiency that made her silently downgrade her own achievement; and negotiate over paying his bill, since she had only a little Greek currency on her, and there was nowhere at hand to exchange her travellers' cheques. By the time he waved goodbye it was almost dark, and Belinda was exhausted.

She drove—slowly, because though the road was properly surfaced it was very narrow and winding—back to the village where she had telephoned, and asked, in the mixture she'd used before of sign language, English, German and the couple of Greek words she'd picked up, for supper at the café.

Omelette and salad, the woman agreed—at least, Belinda thought she agreed. Getting a drink of Coke was easier: she just pointed at a crate in the corner. She took the bottle and a straw, and sat down at a corner table.

She wouldn't have enough money to pay for her supper, she thought guiltily. Oh, well, she'd face that hurdle when she came to it.

It was a small café, rather scruffy, with just half a dozen scuffed formica-topped tables. In one corner was a huge pile of crates full of beer and soft drinks, and in another a vast refrigerator. Elderly calendars and a faded map of the island hung on the walls. Earlier it had been empty, but now a couple of the other tables were occupied by Cretan men. One pair were playing back-gammon, and another man was reading a local paper. The television behind the counter had been switched on to show a football match.

Every few minutes the door opened and another Cretan walked in. They all looked dark and fierce and slightly disreputable. The woman had disappeared, and Belinda was the only female in sight. She began to feel rather uncomfortable. She tried smiling at the men and miming a tyre blowing up, but they shook their heads as if they couldn't understand her. One young man ges-tured to her to join him, but she smiled and shook her head.

A man came out from the back room, talked to some of the customers, and served her another Coke. When she had half drunk it the woman reappeared with bread, cutlery, and a simple salad of tomato and feta.

Was an omelette coming too? Belinda had no idea. The salad had taken long enough, and she was ravenous. She tucked in.

A car flashed past, its headlights glaring against the glass of the café frontage. There was a squeal of brakes. Belinda tore off another piece of bread and continued to eat.

The café door banged. She glanced up—and saw Howard standing there.

Was he an apparition? Hardly: he not only looked very solid, he lookd tired and worried and rather angry.

'Belinda! Thank God!' he declared, striding across to her table.

Belinda jumped to her feet and swallowed her mouthful of bread. She choked, and Howard banged her firmly on the back.

'Thanks,' she spluttered, grabbing the Coke bottle and swallowing a large gulp.

'Not at all,' Howard said with heavy sarcasm. 'For heaven's sake, woman, you must be crazy! You know I've been sick with worry over you?'

'Have you?'

'Of course I damn well have! Do you have any idea what time it is? Well, let me tell you. It's ten o'clock! Ten o'clock, and dark outside, and you're still in the mountains, sitting here as cool as a cucumber eating supper in the crummiest dive in all of Crete!'

'It's a nice salad,' she parried. Howard worried! Had he really been? Judging by his anger—and the fact that he'd tracked her down—he certainly had!

'Damn the salad! It isn't safe to be out on your own in a place like this! Just think what might have happened if I hadn't found you!'

'Nothing! Everyone's been really nice to me. And let me tell you, Howard Henderson, I am *not* a crazy idiot. I had two punctures, I'll have you know. Not one—*two* punctures!'

Howard's eyes opened wide. 'Holy smoke,' he said, and sat down heavily in the nearest chair.

'*And* I changed the wheel all by myself. *And* I managed

to get a repair man to come out straight away. *And*—oh, am I glad to see you!'

'Well, I'm glad to see you too.' He gave her a weary smile, and reached out his hand to take hers.

Belinda squeezed it. The look in Howard's grey eyes was doing very peculiar things to her insides. All the weariness she'd held back seemed to be flooding over her at once, and bringing with it an urge to collapse into his arms and leave him to sort everything out for her.

A sudden loud noise made her tear her eyes away from him. They'd scored a goal on the television. And it had sounded so loud, she suddenly realised, because apart from the television there was silence all across the café—and a dozen or so Cretan men were staring open-mouthed at her and Howard.

Every conversation in the café, every game of back-gammon, must have stopped the moment he had come through the door.

A very inappropriate fit of the giggles came over her.

'What on earth do you think you're——'

'Look at them!' she spluttered. 'We're probably providing the best entertainment they've had here for years.'

'Well, isn't that nice!'

'Don't grouch. You've found me.' And the proprietress was coming through the door at the back, with a plate in her hand. 'Hey, my omelette's coming at last. Want a bit?'

'I've left Gunther in the car.'

'Oh, of course, you must have come with Gunther. Well, go and get him. I'll eat up as fast as I can, but I'm not leaving this.'

'So I see.' He smiled. '*Two* punctures?' he repeated.

'Two. I did mend the first all by myself.'

'Well, good for you.'

'You didn't think I could, did you?'

'To be honest—no.'

She grinned; and Howard grinned too: and then somehow, with the relief of seeing him, she found herself starting to laugh. After a second Howard joined in, and then the pair of men in the corner playing backgammon started to laugh too. Moments later the whole café had erupted in hilarity. They haven't a clue what the joke is, Belinda thought, and that made her laugh even harder.

'You'd better eat that before it gets cold,' Howard finally managed to say. 'Order a couple more, and I'll go and get Gunther.'

'They take ages.'

'Not for us they won't.'

Infuriatingly, this was true. The two men were served beer as soon as they arrived, and omelettes almost before Belinda had finished hers. Gunther explained in German about the two punctures to one of the men playing backgammon. This time they understood, and soon the story had spread round the café, and everybody was smiling and nodding at the three of them.

Greek coffee, very strong and hot and very, very sweet, arrived without their asking for it. Belinda took a sip of hers and sat back, pleasantly full and satisfied. Howard was leaning back too, laughing and gesturing with a piece of bread, holding his beer glass in his other hand. Crummy dive or not, he looked relaxed and happy.

He'd come for her. There he was pretending not to care about her at all, but he must have realised straight away that she was late getting back. And he hadn't waited to see what would happen—he had set out immediately to find her.

He realised her eyes were on him, and turned to look

back at her. Grey eyes, their gaze clear and yet warm, held hers for a long reassuring moment.

I'm in love with him, Belinda thought with weary pleasure. And, for all his casualness, maybe he's just the tiniest bit in love with me too.

'You're not driving back alone,' Howard said gently.

'But I've got to get the car back.'

'I'll drive it, and you can come with me. Gunther will follow us. You don't mind, do you, Gunther?'

'That's OK,' Gunther agreed with a smile. He was getting the thin end of the deal, Belinda thought, but she was too weary to protest strongly. They left the café as soon as Howard had paid for all three of them.

It was a pleasure to subside into the passenger seat, and watch Howard, calm and purposeful, moving back the driver's seat and readjusting the mirrors. It was a pleasure to doze next to him, while he silently drove them back to the hotel. It was a pleasure to let her eyes open now and then, and to see his firm clear profile against the dark Cretan night.

When they got back to the hotel he said determinedly, 'Bed, girl,' and Belinda didn't protest. She didn't even trouble to shower, and her eyes were shut almost before her head touched the pillow.

In spite of the evening's drama, Howard hauled her out of bed for an eight-thirty start the following day. They left the hotel, finished cataloguing his second wild flower site, then continued to drive eastwards until in the early evening they arrived in Agios Nikolaos, one of the biggest resorts on the island.

The resort wasn't busy, and they soon found hotel rooms in the town centre, a couple of blocks inland from the sea, and overlooking a small lake. ·

'Grab a quick shower,' Howard suggested, 'then knock on my door when you're ready for supper.'

And eat with you, Belinda concluded, as she proceeded to take his advice.

Well, why not? The previous evening had done a lot to restore the warmth between them, and she didn't want to go back to eating alone. What was more, she was beginning to think that her hurt, stand-offish attitude had been rather short-sighted.

She didn't really want to end her relationship with Howard, after all. What she wanted was to have a relationship on her terms: a warm, loving relationship that left open the possibility of a growing commitment.

Fun and sex wasn't enough. But Howard was obviously prepared to provide at least a little more than that, as his behaviour the night before had shown. And if she gave their friendship a chance to deepen, wasn't there a possibility that he might come to fully return her own feelings?

It was worth leaving the option open, at least. That didn't mean jumping back into bed with him, but it did mean having suppers together, and perhaps a little gentle—very gentle—prodding to try to persuade him to be more open about his deeper thoughts and feelings.

Nothing too sexy, then, she decided, as she rifled through her suitcase. She finally unearthed a yellow and blue striped cotton skirt that came to just below her knees, and a yellow knit cotton top with a high round neck. It really did need *some* jewellery, but she tried to keep it light, with just an armful of bangles and a couple of long thin gold chains looped around her neck.

'Hi,' Howard said, as he opened his door to her. 'I'm on the balcony, just drinking an ouzo. Like to join me?'

'If mine can be orange juice,' she agreed. One sip of the anise-based Greek aperitif had been enough for her.

'I've a carton in the sink, cooling.'

As he was getting it she drifted out on to his balcony, and stared down at the dark green waters of the lake.

'Lake Voulismeni,' Howard said, appearing at her side with their drinks in his hands. 'A bottomless pool.'

'I can believe it.' The lake was beautiful but also slightly sinister, with heavy cliffs overhanging the far side, and that deep, opaque water.

'Well, not literally. Actually it's about sixty-four metres deep, but that's more than enough water to drown in. And cold—I wouldn't recommend you to take a dip.'

'I don't plan to. Anyway, I'm starving, so I hope we can eat soon. Are we eating here?'

'I thought not. Agios Nikolaos has some of the best restaurants in Crete, so we'll see if we can find something really special.'

'Sounds good.'

'You deserve it. You've worked hard today.' He put his drink down, set his hands on her shoulders, and dropped a light kiss on her forehead. 'Drink up and we'll get moving.'

She didn't want to drink up for a moment. She wanted to savour his touch. She wanted another kiss. Oh-oh, she admonished herself. Don't give in too easily. You've got to renegotiate terms first!

And wasn't this another sign that Howard too was beginning to reconsider his attitude?

They ate in a restaurant just along from their hotel, overlooking the cool waters of the lake. It was a simple but very good meal, a seafood starter followed by an excellent steak, plus the inevitable Greek salad. Howard ordered an expensive bottle of Cretan wine, and they drank slowly, savouring the rich red liquid.

Belinda didn't want to frighten him off by asking personal questions too quickly, and while they waited for their food they chatted about the flowers, about Gunther and the other tourists they had met, and about the tourist attractions within reach of their new base.

Coffee came, and Belinda said casually, 'I finished my postcards over lunch yesterday, all twenty-seven of them. I misjudged slightly and bought thirty stamps, so can I pass the spare ones on to you?'

'If you like. I'll probably need them some time.'

'If you've done all your postcards, then do tell me. I'm not trying to make you buy them if you can't use them.'

'I don't send postcards on your scale, Belinda.'

'You must send some! To your parents? Your aunts and uncles? Friends back at the University?'

'Perhaps I should send a few.'

'Don't you usually? Don't your parents expect to get one from you?'

'Not everyone has a family precisely like yours.'

'Of course not, but. . .' But everybody loves their parents and wants to keep in close touch, she meant to say; only it struck her then that this perhaps wasn't true of Howard. 'Do your parents live in Melchester?' she asked instead.

'No, they live in a suburb of Bradford.'

'So do you see them often?'

'It depends what you call often. I suppose I go up there once or twice a year.'

Once or twice a *year*! Bradford was perhaps a hundred

miles from Melchester, so a visit would mean an overnight stay. But even so, it seemed to her to be alarmingly
little.

'What do they do?'

'My father works for an insurance company.'

'Selling insurance, you mean? Or managing an office,
or what?'

'He's a clerk—nothing exciting.'

'And your mother? Does she work?'

'She's a psychologist.'

'That sounds interesting.'

'It seems to interest her.'

'What does she do? Talk to patients, or advise com-
panies, or what? Does she see children? I should think
it'd be fascinating, being a child psychologist.'

'I think it's mainly adults.'

'So she analyses their minds, sort of?'

'I really don't know. She doesn't discuss her work.'

Like mother, like son, Belinda added silently. But at
least he was answering her now, and though she felt as
if she was living on borrowed time, she was determined
to persist for as long as he let her.

'Your mum's more successful than your dad, then?'

'It depends what you call successful. I think they both
do their jobs competently. I suppose Mother earns rather
more than Father does.'

'Does that bother them?'

'Obviously it bo—look, this is really none of your
business.'

'I didn't mean to pry, Howard—I'm just interested.
People interest me. What they do, how they get on with
each other, the things that they agree about and the
things that they argue about, all of that fascinates me.'

'Some people prefer to maintain some privacy.'

'Of course everybody wants *some* privacy. Nobody wants everybody else to know everything about them. But everybody needs to be close to a few other people, to feel that they can tell them everything. That's what life is about, isn't it?'

'Not necessarily.'

'Oh, I think it is! It makes things so much easier. When things are going well you need somebody to be pleased with you, and when things are going badly you need somebody to share your troubles. Like when you came to rescue me yesterday.'

'I hardly think that compares with my parents' disagreements.'

'Maybe that wasn't the best example.' Belinda had a silent think for a moment. Then she took a deep breath, and said, 'Well, take last week, for instance. I was really upset when we had that row, so I went back to the hotel and had a good howl, and then in the morning I wrote a card to Charmian—that's my sister. You know— Howard Henderson's a pig and I'm miserable and I'll tell you all about it when I get home. Mind you, writing a card isn't quite the same as telling Charmian properly and having her tell me it's not so bad after all, but it helps. It's not all bottled up inside me, I know there's somebody I can have a good grouch to.'

'I think that's humiliating.'

'For you or for me?' She grinned.

'Well, for you especially. Not that I particularly want to be called a pig on a postcard, but for you to write it, I meant.'

'Didn't you have a good grouch to anyone when Deirdre went off and got married to somebody else?'

'Of course not!'

'Oh, Howard!'

Her warm rush of sympathy was too strong to be contained. How *awful* it must be, it seemed to her, to be like Howard! How miserable, to keep all one's troubles to oneself, and have no shoulder to cry on when things went wrong.

'That's how I choose to live my life,' Howard said coolly. 'Now, would you like another coffee here, or shall we go and look for a café down by the harbour?'

'I'm fine here. And you're not wriggling away like that, Howard Henderson. It's no good changing the subject whenever anyone starts asking you personal questions. Don't you have any men friends? Don't you talk to them?'

'Men don't talk about that sort of thing.'

'Of course they do!'

'A lot you know about it!'

'I know more than you might think. My dad talks to all of us at home, about things at work and so on. He doesn't tell us about his clients, obviously, because he's not allowed to, but he talks about rows with the senior partner and problems with his secretary and that kind of thing. My boyfriend Paul used to talk to me all the time. And Charmian's boyfriend talks to her, and a couple of boys I know from college come round and tell me about their troubles with their girlfriends, and— honestly, everybody does it.'

'That's not so. Perhaps your friends do, but my friends don't.'

'Because they're scared of being humiliated?'

'Don't be ridiculous, Belinda. Waiter! Two coffees, please.'

'I don't think that's ridiculous,' Belinda persisted. 'I think it's very important. It's as if you hide away from the world, Howard, for fear it's going to laugh at you or hurt you in some way. The way you act and talk and dress and everything about you, it's all hiding away. Other people aren't that horrible, you know. You want to open up to them more, and you'll find they're really nice.'

'Like you, I suppose? With your trashy sentimental pop music and your come-on clothes and your way of chatting up every stranger who crosses your path? Well, I don't want to be like that, and I won't have you making out that I should!'

Trashy sentiment! Was that really how he saw her honest, straightforward feelings? A hot flush of humiliation washed over Belinda's face. If most people behaved as Howard did, it would be no wonder if others learned to hide behind protective shells!

'It isn't trash to me,' she managed to say in a brightish voice. But the spirit had gone out of the conversation, and it was all she could do to be polite to him until the waiter came with their bill.

More days went by. Belinda had learned plenty about the local wild flowers by now. Much of the work of cataloguing each site was repetitive, but she could see from Howard's records how the pattern of growth on each site was changing, and she found it interesting, as well as rather alarming, to discover how worldwide pollution was affecting this remote island as well as more obviously industrial areas.

They generally parted when they returned to their hotel, spending the early evening alone and meeting up again for supper, when they sometimes joined other couples staying in the area, before saying goodnight early to each other.

Belinda finished her store of romances, and borrowed

a couple of Howard's thrillers to read. Howard bought an English newspaper every other day, and if they were eating alone they puzzled over the crossword together.

They made great efforts to be polite to each other. Howard didn't again criticise her taste in books, music and clothes, and she didn't make any further effort to pry into his thoughts and feelings. Feelings? What feelings? It seemed to her that he didn't know what feelings were.

After a week they left Agios Nikolaos and went to stay in Sitia, a smaller resort to the far east of the island, with a big harbour and a Moorish ruined castle on the clifftop above. Slowly the weather improved again. Both of them were deeply tanned now, and Belinda fell into the habit of swimming briefly each afternoon when they returned to the town.

Howard didn't swim with her, but she discovered— by chance, when a tourist with whom they were dining let drop a comment—that he too had a daily swim, before breakfast.

It should have been an idyllic existence: living under sunny skies, doing interesting work, eating well and drinking wine each evening, meeting and talking to strangers. But it wasn't. The strain of behaving casually to Howard seemed to weigh more and more heavily on her. She willed her stronger feelings for him to fade away, but they stubbornly failed to do it to order. Again and again she caught herself reaching out to him. She was forced to censor each word, each move, in order to keep up the façade of friendly indifference that he appeared to maintain so effortlessly.

'Would you mind working tomorrow?' Howard asked one Friday, as they were returning from a new site up in the mountains. 'I'd really like to get this site finished while it's fresh in our minds. It's the last one at this end of the island, so we could take Sunday and Monday off, and then see about moving westwards.'

'You don't have to give me Monday off.'

'I think I should. I've been working you hard, and you deserve a proper weekend of sorts.'

'I don't much like the weekends.' She said it automatically, then she could have kicked herself! She always tried to give Howard the impression that she had a whale of a time when she wasn't with him. But it wasn't true, and all she could think of now was getting home to England—away from him, and back to the love and companionship of her family and friends.

Howard didn't reply immediately. Belinda drove on. Then he said, in a casual voice, 'I'd like to go to Vai before we set off west. You haven't been there yet, have you? Maybe we could go together on Sunday.'

'What's at Vai? More heaps of stone?'

'No. Of course there are archaeological sites close by—there are everywhere in Crete, you know that!— but Vai isn't famous for them. It's just a pleasant bay, with a grove of palm trees and a sheltered beach. It's good for swimming. I thought we might have a lazy day for once, swim and sunbathe and have a long lunch at the taverna by the beach.'

'Sounds nice.'

'Could you stand my company, then?'

'There's nobody else's, is there?'

She knew it sounded petty and resentful. And when Howard didn't respond she made an effort, and continued, 'I'm sorry, that was mean. Thank you, I'd like your company.'

'OK. we'll do that on Sunday, and then talk then about what we should do on Monday.'

Vai was remote, even by Cretan standards. The tiny bay was more than half an hour's drive from Sitia, and there was no other town nearby. Nor were there any hotels at the bay, though there was, as Howard had said, a taverna on the beach. A collection of coaches in the car park attested to the fame of the little bay, and the fact that it was regarded as a 'must' for visitors to Crete.

It was easy to see why. A grove of palm trees, rare on the island, wove down a broad valley, and erupted on to a fine sandy beach. A little island sheltered the bay from the easterly winds, and there were pleasant walks up the cliffs on either side of the bay.

For a moment, gazing at the sight in front of her, Belinda could forget her tension and feel nothing but sheer pleasure at being on the island.

'Lovely, isn't it?' Howard said softly.

'It really is.' She turned to him and, for a moment, allowed herself simply to gaze at him. In shorts and a white shirt that he had already half unbuttoned to show off his muscular torso, his tan deepened to cork colour, he looked devastatingly attractive.

How perfect it all could have been, if only he were able to return her feelings! While as it was, being here with him was a kind of exquisite torture: so nearly what she wanted, and yet so infinitely remote from it.

His eyes caught and held hers, and, with a pang, she made herself look away. Why did he have to look at her like that? His look seemed to say so clearly that he wanted her, that he felt it was only her silly scruples, her asking for too much, that were keeping them apart. But it wasn't like that at all! It was him, his inability to feel, to love, to take her and her feelings seriously, that formed the real barrier between them.

'Coming to swim?' he asked.

'Nope, too cold.' Belinda made her way out of the shade of the palms to a clear sunny stretch of sand, and dropped her bathing mat and the bag containing her towel, paperback and sunglasses. 'I'm having a lazy day today. Just wake me when it's time to go home.'

'The sea's a little warmer here than off most of the beaches. Have a go.'

'Later, maybe.'

'I'll give you half a hour,' he conceded. 'Put some suntan lotion on—the sun's stronger than you think.'

'And my tan isn't as good as yours.'

'Shall I do your back for you?'

'No, thanks, I'll do it myself.'

She busied herself with the bottle of lotion, doing her best to ignore Howard, barely a couple of paces away, stripping off his shorts and shirt. Though that wasn't easy, and once he'd moved off down the beach she let her eyes follow him as she strode towards the sea.

She'd get over it, she told herself brutally. One day there would come a time, surely, when her insides didn't clench with desire each time she looked at him. Maybe one day she would even find another man who could make her feel like this. But meanwhile, she had got to tread carefully, or being with him would be even more unbearable than it already was.

He paused for a moment at the water's edge, and she forced herself to turn on to her stomach and settle down to doze in the sunshine.

She was woken again by a splash of something cold on the small of her back.

'Oh, no!' she groaned.

'Oh, yes,' Howard's voice responded. 'Time's up. I'm not going to be the only one who's freezing! Come and swim out to the island.'

Belinda gave him a sideways glance. His feet were just by her head, and her eyes travelled upwards up sinewy legs, past brief black swimming trunks. Droplets of seawater gleamed among the thick mat of hair on his chest. Its shadow traced a fainter V down the flat surface of his stomach.

'Too far.' She turned over again, to shut that disturbingly masculine figure out of her vision. But he wouldn't be dismissed. He shook another faint shower of water over her, and when she shrieked and curled away he reached out to grab her hand and pull her upright.

'Chase you to the water!'

Even cold water would be better than the electric shock of his hand. He wasn't going to leave her alone until she'd been in, so she might as well get it over with. She pulled her hand away, took a couple of faltering steps, then, as he broke into a run, gathered her energy and chased after him. She didn't reach him by the time he was splashing through the shallows, but she waded onwards, through cool water that gradually deepened until she could swim, out to sea, towards the distant island, after the arrow-shape that was Howard, streaking efficiently through the water.

He swam too fast for her, and soon she gave up trying to catch him, and eased into a slow breast-stroke and finally into treading water. The bay was shallow, and though she was well out from the shore she sensed that she was barely out of her depth. Howard was right: the water here was a little warmer than elsewhere on the island. But it was still too cold to be comfortable, and it

was a relief to see him pause, turn, and come swimming
back to her.

'Too far for you?' he called.

'At this temperature it is. Bring me back in August
and I'll swim out there with you.'

'We'll be in England then, writing up my research.
Come on, let's get back to the shore and I'll buy you an
ice-cream.'

'Are you trying to freeze me solid?' But her protest
was teasing, and she stayed by his side as they swam
back to shallower water, then waded ashore through the
shallows together.

CHAPTER SEVEN

INSTEAD of an ice-cream they settled for a drink: ouzo for Howard, gin and tonic for Belinda, which they drank sitting on the terrace of the beach taverna. Belinda was still exhilarated from the cold swim, and feeling almost high from her awareness of Howard's semi-naked body so close to hers.

He reached over and put a hand over the ones she had clasped together on the table. A shiver ran through her. Had he noticed? she wondered uneasily. Or did he take it for an effect of the cold? She didn't dare to pull her hands away, for fear he'd read into the gesture all the true intensity of her reaction to his touch.

Today was the first time he'd touched her even casually for over a week. He hadn't made any attempt to get her back into his bed, but she was conscious that his desire for her still lay just under the surface of their relationship. And if he realised how responsive she was to his touch, how badly she wanted him, he might well be tempted to try again. . .

No. She couldn't afford that; she didn't trust herself to keep him at arm's length if he made a serious attempt to come closer again. Their present relationship was agony, but to drift back into an affair on his terms would be a thousand times worse. She willed her hands to keep still, to appear indifferent to the warm weight of his.

'If we eat early,' he said, 'then I can have another ouzo with lunch. There'll be plenty of time to sober up before we have to make our way back.'

'You're driving back? I will, if you prefer.'

'No way. This isn't a working day, so the normal rules apply. Driving's a man's job.'

'A man's job? Are you trying to tell me, Howard Henderson, that you think you're a better driver than I am?'

'Would I dare?' he laughed. His eyes searched for hers again, but she was careful not to meet them. 'No, I was just giving you a chance to opt out for once, and have a glass of wine with your lunch. Now, shall we order?'

They did. Belinda didn't really want to drink wine: her resistance to him was at such a low ebb already that she knew it would be dangerous to lower her inhibitions any further. But she didn't want to refuse his suggestion either, and make him wonder why, so she allowed him to order her a glass—and then a second.

The terrace was pleasantly shady, and the view looking out over the bay was glorious. The wine slipped down easily. The afternoon grew hot and mellow. A couple of large coach parties had left the bay, and it was now quite quiet, though a few children splashed about at the edge of the sea.

'You know what I'm going to do after lunch?' Belinda asked dreamily.

'Swim again?'

'With all this alcohol in me? No fear! No, I'm going to go back to the car and fetch my Walkman. Then I'm going to plug in my earphones and play my favourite Madonna tape to myself very loudly. I'm going to oil myself all over again, and lie on my back, and fall asleep in the sun.'

'Sounds promising, though I'd prefer to listen to the Velvet Underground myself.'

'Too bad. If you like I'll leave the earphones off, and you can listen to Madonna too.'

'No fear.'

'Now, what's wrong with Madonna?'

He shrugged. It was a casual gesture, but she sensed that it was charged with tautness.

He feels the same, she thought with sudden insight. He wants me just as badly as I want him. It's torture for him too to hold back all the time.

Her stand-off tactics might keep her out of the wrong kind of relationship with Howard, but that was all they were doing, she thought to herself—with the artificial clarity that the wine had induced in her. That wasn't what she wanted. What she wanted was to break down those damned defences of his—and wasn't this the ideal moment to try?

Recklessly, she changed tactics and went on the attack.

'Seriously, Howard, what do you have against my taste in pop music? Or sorry, should I call it "sentimental slush"?'

'That's what it is, isn't it? There's no depth to it. Just that mindless pounding beat, and empty lyrics about love and heartache.'

'The beat's good. It doesn't take any thought, true, but that's the point of it. It appeals to the animal instinct in all of us. It's the rhythm of life itself. And as for empty lyrics, that's just ridiculous. What's so meaningless about love and heartache? It's a basic human experience.'

'Howling about it isn't a basic human experience. It's sheer self-indulgence, if you ask me. I don't think people ought to publicise their feelings in such a sloppy way.

True art consists of decent restraint, not of letting it all hang out.'

'You talk as if it's a crime! I don't understand, Howard. It's not *wrong* to want to share your feelings with other people. It's something we all need to do. You talk about restraining your feelings, but when it comes down to it, I'm not sure that you have any to restrain!'

'And you think *that's* a crime, don't you? Because I live a sensible well-balanced life and don't go in for great dramas and agonies you seem to think there's something missing in me.'

'In that sense there is.'

The sudden surge of anger that brought him rising from his chair took her by surprise, but she was just quick enough to catch at his wrist and pull him back down. 'Don't be silly,' she said. 'I mean—well, it's hard to explain. Look, Howard, you have to understand that I hurt. It really hurts me that you don't love me the way I love you. I suppose it would hurt worse if you loved somebody else instead, but it hurts to think that you don't love anybody. In a funny way it's as if you *can't* love anybody.'

If she'd been sober she would have known that she was pushing him too far, but she was beyond noticing the danger signs: the darkness in his grey eyes, the anger in his lowered brows. But he held himself back, and when he replied it was in a calm, if chilly, voice.

'You don't understand me at all, Belinda. You don't have the vaguest idea what I think.'

'Think? Oh, I reckon I know what you think. You think I'm young and silly and my dresses are too short and I wear too much jewellery. All that's no news to me. But what I can't understand is how you *feel*, Howard. Not thoughts: feelings. The two are different, you know.'

'Has it never occurred to you,' Howard said icily, 'that I hurt too?'

It hadn't. She hadn't believed he was capable of feeling hurt, least of all over her. And even now, stumbling to steer a course between her hurt and her anger and her desire to understand, she couldn't figure out what he meant.

'I do have needs too,' Howard was going on, his voice harsh and oddly insistent. 'Maybe I don't pour my heart out to every passing stranger, but that doesn't mean I'm not human. How do you think *I* felt when you decided to stop sleeping with me? Do you think it didn't matter to me? Do you think I didn't *mind?*'

'Well. . . Not in the way that. . .'

'Not in your way, true. I don't understand that sloppy undisciplined emotion you call "love". I don't believe in looking for another person so that I can open the floodgates and let everything that's in me, good and bad, spew out in a messy emotional flood. But I do believe in desire, Belinda, and liking, and the need to be close to other people, physically and mentally, from time to time.'

'From time to time!'

'I wanted us to go on, Belinda. All right, we fell into bed too fast, but we both know how well it worked for us. I was damn sorry when you finished it. And why did you finish it? Because you were looking for a mirage! Real commitments, real desire, weren't enough for you, were they? You wanted the kind of faked-up, larger-than-life emotion you hear about in your rubbishy pop songs. And I wouldn't fake it like that.'

'But it's not faked!' Belinda yelled back. 'That's what you don't understand, Howard! It's not hyped-up and insincere, it's how people feel! People *do* go crazy over one another when they fall in love! They don't fancy a little bit of intimacy from time to time, they want to be with the other person *all* the time! They *want* to share everything with the other person! And when it goes wrong, it isn't a little itchy pain like a mosquito bite. They bleed. Do you understand that, Howard? They bleed!'

'Well, I don't want to bleed!'

'Nobody wants to bleed! But don't you see? You can't be truly happy without opening yourself out to other people. And if it goes wrong, that makes you truly unhappy. That's the risk you take if you want to be fully alive. You don't bottle everything up inside you, you don't live behind a wall. You don't think in terms of opening the floodgates, because in a healthy person there *are* no floodgates!'

'That's just not true!'

'It is! It is! You just can't see it, because you're so inhibited that you can't imagine what it's like to be any different.'

'Don't you think it's maybe that *you're* so self-indulgent that you can't understand what it's like to control your own feelings?'

'What else do you think I've been doing for the last fortnight?'

There was an instant when he was lost for a reply: only an instant, but it was long enough. Belinda had swept to her feet, crashed her chair back under the table, and dashed in a headlong rush from the taverna before he had time to move.

She ran at random: anywhere, just to get away from him. Indeed, to get away from everyone—all the holidaymakers with their reddened bodies and their sunshades and their curious glances. Up the cliff path she ran, swerving instinctively to avoid the people coming down it, and keeping her eyes from theirs. Past the cliff-top, where there was a tourist shelter overlooking the bay; onwards, over the rough ground, towards the next bay, forwards, anywhere, just to be alone!

She had no idea how long she ran. But at last she was so out of breath that she had to pause, and take some thick, gasping breaths to fill her lungs again.

The bay and the palm forest were out of sight. All the holidaymakers were far behind her. Howard was far behind her too. She thought for a terrible, exhilarating moment that he might come after her; but no. He wasn't a man for grand emotional scenes. He'd much more likely wait until she calmed down and stopped being crazy and undisciplined and hysterical. Then he'd greet her coolly when she came back, and pretend that the whole incident had never happened.

He didn't hurt like this. He couldn't. He didn't love her. He didn't understand about feelings at all.

And oh, hers were raw! She felt as if she had been flayed from top to toe. She had never felt this kind of pain before. She had never loved like this before, and never been rejected before; not like this, by a man who seemed to despise everything that meant most to her.

It hurt almost too much to bear. She subsided to the ground and wrapped her arms around herself. It was as if she could feel the pain retreating inwards, nestling around her heart, making a hot aching place deep inside her.

She wasn't used to being wounded; she wasn't used to feeling vulnerable. She had always faced the world cheerfully and openly, and the world had always greeted her in the same spirit. She'd sometimes been disappointed, but only in little ways. She had never before

longed desperately for anything without getting it. Now
she longed: for Howard to come running over the hill-
top and tell her that he loved her the way she loved him,
and wanted to give her all that she wanted and needed
from him. Yet at the same time she knew that it wouldn't
happen.

She sat there for a long time. She didn't know how to
go back and face him again. How stupid she had been!
He had already known how she felt, so why had she
blundered on, spelling it out to him all over again, when
it had been obvious from the first that he didn't feel the
same way about her?

It only made it worse that he had confessed to hurting
in his little way, to caring a little bit for her. What use
was his modest amount of lust and liking, when set
against the whirlwind of her emotions? It was an insult,
a travesty, a cruel mockery of all that she wanted from
him. She gave and asked for love, and what was he
offering? A few friendly impersonal conversations and
sex on demand? No, thank you!

Eventually she began to feel that she couldn't sit there
any longer. She got to her feet and began to walk. She
wasn't ready yet to go back to the bay, so she walked in
the other direction, over rough grass, through drifts of
spring flowers like those she and Howard had catalogued
so carefully.

She came to the next bay. There were only a couple of
holidaymakers there, their pitch staked out by towels
and mats on the coarse sand. She walked on. She was
beginning to feel hot and thirsty and tired. She turned
and walked back to the bay. She slipped off her beach
wrap and the loose sandals she had worn to lunch in the
taverna, and waded into the cold water.

She swam for a long time, longer than she had swum

with Howard that morning, until the chill of the water
began to seep into her bones and she couldn't stand the
clean ache of it any longer. Then she waded ashore,
subdued and emotionally exhausted, and slowly made
her way back to the main bay.

She saw Howard when she reached the shelter on the
clifftop. He was down below her, still sitting where she
had left him on the terrace of the taverna. His sun-
bleached hair looked almost yellow in the afternoon
light, his bare torso a deep even mahogany. He was
reading the book he had brought with him that morning.

The iceberg. What an insult it was, for him to suggest
that he had feelings that rivalled hers!

Belinda approached him cautiously, reluctantly, her
hurt a cold lump in her stomach. When she set foot on
the terrace he glanced across at her. Warily, he watched
her come up to him.

'I need a coffee,' she said quietly.

'I'll order you one.'

They left—without discussion—on Monday. Neither of
them wanted another day of leisure. They breakfasted in
silence, then set out on the long slow drive westwards.

Howard drove. He didn't linger and look for flowers:
he just drove, as fast as possible, without stopping any
more than was strictly necessary. Belinda sat next to
him, headphones clamped to her ears, listening to pop
music. She meant it to provide some consolation, but it
didn't. The oozing emotions of the singers on her tapes
somehow didn't echo her own feelings. Instead they
seemd to mock them.

It was mid-afternoon when they arrived at
Rethimnon, a pretty town on the north coast of the
island, with a harbour dominated by a lighthouse and a

huge Venetian fort. They found a small hotel overlooking
the beach. Howard disappeared into his room without
making any comment about meeting up for supper, and
Belinda didn't notice this omission until she was under
the shower.

Just as well, she thought viciously. She wouldn't have
spent the evening with that block of ice if he were the
last man on Crete! She spent a desultory half-hour
unpacking a few of her clothes. It was still only four-
thirty. I'll explore the town, she decided.

Really she didn't feel like looking at shops, though;
and she barely even noticed the charming houses of the
old quarter with their overhanging wooden balconies,
and the elegant buildings from the era when the
Venetians had ruled Crete. She walked at random down
side-streets and main streets: anywhere, just so long as
she didn't see Howard.

Finally she came out, rather to her surprise, on to the
harbour. She circled around it, heading for the promon-
tory with its great fort.

She hadn't really thought of looking around the fort,
so it wasn't a great disappointment when she learned
that it was closed on Mondays. It did kill the last of her
half-hearted interest in sightseeing, though, and instead,
in a subdued mood, she retraced her steps to the
harbourside. She picked at random one of the café tables
on the pavement, sat down, and ordered a lemonade.

'Belinda!'

Howard! The thought jerked her into alertness. But
she knew immediately that it wasn't Howard's voice. It
did sound familiar, though. . .of course! There was
Gunther, threading his way through the tables towards
her.

'Gunther! I didn't know you were in Rethimnon.'

'Nor I that you were. May I join you?'

'Please do.'

He took a seat opposite hers, and waved to the waiter. He insisted on cancelling her lemonade, and instead ordered a bottle of wine for them to share.

'You are alone?' he asked curiously. 'Howard is not here?'

'He's back at the hotel.' Belinda described, briefly, their drive that day, and her sudden decision to go sightseeing on her own.

'So you go back to your hotel next, and eat with Howard?'

'We hadn't arranged anything.'

Gunther raised his brows, and on impulse Belinda went on, 'To be honest, we tend to see too much of each other. We work together all day, and then there isn't really anybody else to see in the evenings, so we tend to eat together as well. It's a pleasure when we meet up with somebody else.'

'For you, maybe: but if I were Dr Henderson, I think that I would never want any company other than yours.'

Gunther's manner, rather to her embarrassment, was as flirtatious as his words. She gave him a bright, empty smile to acknowledge the compliment, but she avoided his eyes. She didn't want him to get the wrong impression!

'Oh, I don't know,' she said casually. 'Even the best-matched couples need other people's company from time to time, and Howard and I are hardly one of those.'

'You think not? I had wondered if perhaps. . .'

'No, not at all.'

'So that decides us. You eat with me this evening. Now shall we eat here, or shall we go into the old town, or out to one of the hotels along by the beach?'

Oops! She hadn't really been fishing for an invitation, though she could see now that Gunther was justified in assuming that she had been. She had still had a half idea in her mind of returning to the hotel and seeking out Howard.

But that would have been a very bad idea, she acknowledged to herself. Nor could she politely refuse Gunther now. Anyway, why should she refuse him? He was pleasant, interesting company, and even good-looking in a rather lugubrious way. It should be a great improvement on eating alone.

'Let's eat here.'

'I'll ask for the menu.'

This done, he drew his chair closer to Belinda's, leaned towards her, and said, 'So tell me about yourself.'

Oops, again. Gunther had been casually friendly, no more, when Howard was around, but now he was acting positively interested. And Howard or no Howard, she really wasn't interested in him in the same way. She moved her chair just a fraction away from his, and kept her manner as cool as it was bright as she told him a few snippets about her family and background. Then she politely asked him about his.

The waiter brought bread, salad and grilled prawns. Belinda talked, and Gunther talked. Gunther moved closer; Belinda retreated; Gunther moved closer again, and this time she found that her chair was jammed up against the table leg.

The waiter brought grilled red mullet, and Gunther insisted on helping her remove the bones. He was attentive and flattering, and he kept leaning over so that he was very close to her, in a way that she found more annoying than arousing.

The waiter cleared their empty plates. Gunther asked

him for more wine. Belinda glanced at the empty bottle in astonishment. She had been monitoring her own drinking carefully, and had not yet finished her first glass, so it was Gunther who had drunk the rest of the bottle.

'What pretty rings you wear,' he said now, reaching out and taking her hand.

'I'm glad you like them.' She smiled to soften the gesture as she wriggled her hand away. But he tightened his grip just in time, and her wriggle didn't free it from his.

'This one here, it is most unusual.'

'It's from India.'

'Pretty, very pretty. And it's a pretty woman who wears them.' He lifted her hand to his mouth, lightly kissed the back of it, then turned it over and kissed the palm.

'Please don't do that, Gunther.'

'But with a pretty woman, one wants to do that.'

'I'd rather you didn't.' She pulled her hand away, decisively this time. 'It's dark,' she went on hurriedly. 'I really ought to be getting back to the hotel.'

'Not yet. Look, there's more wine coming. Have another glass.'

'Oh, no, I've drunk plenty already.'

'Then sit with me while I drink some more. Coffee?'

'Well. . .just quickly, perhaps.'

Gunther refilled his glass. His hand shook slightly, and some of the wine splashed on to the table-top. He was rather sozzled already, and most of the new bottle of wine was still waiting to be drunk. It struck Belinda that it might be sensible to leave him after having her coffee, and walk back to the hotel alone.

It was dark, though, and the hotel was quite a long

way away, and she wasn't even absolutely sure of the route. Perhaps she should ask for a taxi?

'You don't have a boyfriend, do you?' Gunther said suddenly. 'Come back to my hotel with me tonight.'

'Gunther!' She jumped to her feet, pushing aside her half-empty coffee cup. 'I'm going back to my hotel. Thank you for dinner,' she went on self-consciously. 'It really was delicious.'

'Don't go yet. There's more wine still.'

'I know, but I've drunk more than enough already. You stay and finish it. I'll ask the waiter to find me a taxi.'

'You stay too.' Gunther lumbered to his feet, and caught her hands in his. 'Pretty B'linda, sit down again.'

'No, Gunther, really. Gunther, please let me go. Let me go!'

Their disagreement was turning into a tussle, and one or two diners at other tables were staring openly at them. Belinda flushed with embarrassment. Gunther was tall and strong, and no longer sober enough to be sensible. She fought to free her hands, and glanced around rather desperately, hoping that someone, the waiter perhaps, would come to her assistance.

'Pretty B'linda. Pretty sexy B'linda. Tease, aren't you? All short skirts and giggles, but when you ask for it, it isn't there. Is that what you and Howard rowed about? Because you led him on and wouldn't give it to him?'

'Gunther!' With a final desperate shake, Belinda freed herself. She grabbed her shoulderbag from the back of the chair, and dashed down the harbourside.

At first she was terrified that Gunther would chase her. She was wearing her high-heeled white sandals, and she couldn't run properly over the uneven pavement. But she hurried as much as she could, and soon she felt

sure that he wasn't coming. The wine had probably won
out over her as an attraction!

When she reached the far end of the harbour she felt
safe enough to pause and catch her breath. It was
definitely dark now, and there was only a smattering of
people about. It wouldn't be sensible to walk back to the
hotel. She made for another harbourside restaurant, and
asked the waiter to call her a taxi.

The Howard who greeted her in the hotel dining-room
next morning looked extremely grumpy. 'Where did you
get to last night?' he barked, before she had a chance to
say anything to him. 'I knocked on your door and looked
in the bar and on the beach, but you weren't anywhere.'

Belinda shrugged. So what if she hadn't been there?
Howard didn't own her, and she had a perfect right to
spend her evenings away from him.

She didn't have to take this kind of behaviour from
him, she thought irritably. She could always walk away,
and breakfast alone at another table.

That would have been rather short-sighted, though,
when she was going to have to work with him all day.
So she pulled out the chair opposite his, saying offhandedly, 'I went for a walk. And then I met Gunther, so I
had supper with him.'

'Gunther?'

'That's what I said. He arrived here yesterday.'

From Howard's intensified scowl, it was obvious that
this explanation didn't please him. Too bad, she thought
mutinously. It only served him right if he'd wasted time
looking for her and then had to eat alone. Why should
he expect her to keep him company?

Because you've been doing just that up to now, a little

voice in her head whispered. But she wasn't in a mood to be fair to him.

Nor was Howard in a mood for another argument, though. With a visible effort he put aside his ill-temper, and said in a cool but polite voice, 'Sit down. We don't want to be late starting work.'

Belinda sat, and when the waitress came over they ordered coffee and rolls.

'It would be good to see Gunther again,' Howard said. 'Where's he staying?'

'How am I to know?'

This answer brought a stare of surprise to him: and to her, the guilty realisation that she was being extremely rude. But the waitress brought their breakfast just then, so the awkward scene that threatened was avoided, and they settled for eating their breakfast in silence.

They started out in silence too, driving along the main road that led west, hugging the coast. But Belinda couldn't stand the heavy atmosphere for long, and soon she asked Howard to play some music. The snappy beat of Michael Jackson fitted her tense mood, and she enjoyed it, even if Howard's face remained hard-set in a semi-scowl.

They took a small road that led up into the high mountains that formed the island's backbone, and began to search for Howard's next wild flower site.

'It's here, I think,' he said as they rounded a bend on the narrow track.

'Sure?'

'No. But stop and I'll check.'

Belinda braked. She stayed in the car while Howard got out and ventured down the steep hillside.

He was gone fifteen minutes or more. Then he reappeared, looking hot and exasperated, and said,

'Sorry, this can't be it. I can't find the markers anywhere. You'd better drive on.'

'Where to?'

'Up the road somewhere. I don't know; there must be
somewhere else that looks similar.'

Belinda sighed. It was going to be one of those days.
As soon as Howard's seat-belt was fastened she set off,
with a protesting grumble from the engine.

She was halfway round the next blind bend when she
saw a car coming in the opposite direction. She braked
sharply, and stopped just inches from its bumper.

'Oh, blow it!'

'Back up a bit,' Howard said.

'There's nowhere to pass back there.'

'You'll have to go right round the bend.'

'I'm not backing round a hairpin bend with a drop
like that at the side of the road. Why can't he back
instead?'

'I told you to back,' Howard said curtly.

'And I'm telling you I'm not.' Belinda stared at the
car facing them. A dour-looking Cretan stared back at
her, and gestured to her to reverse her car. She made the
same gesture impatiently back at him.

'Oh, for heaven's sake, get out and I'll back it!'
snapped Howard.

'I will not!' With an emphatically angry gesture, she
wrenched the gears into reverse and began to edge
around the bend.

The Cretan followed her, nose to nose. Belinda was
determined not to edge too near to the drop, so she
backed up close to the rocks on the inside of the road,
and soon the other car squeezed past her, and was gone
in a cloud of dust.

'Wait here a minute,' Howard said.

'It's a blind bend, for heaven's sake!'

'I won't be long.' He opened the door, and slammed it behind him.

He was going to check on some flowers! Curse him! All the time she had been inching backwards on the mountain road, he'd been watching the roadside for unusual plants. The insensitive, unsympathetic boor! Belinda clenched her hands on the steering-wheel, and uttered a large number of unpleasant epithets under her breath.

'No, it's not,' Howard said shortly, getting back into the car.

'Might have guessed,' Belinda muttered.

She drove on. Twice they came to places broadly similar to the first one where they had stopped, with rocky grassland sloping away not too steeply to her left. Each time she stopped and Howard went to hunt for the markers; each time he failed to find them.

'You must have the wrong road,' she said unsympathetically, when he returned, shrugging, to the car for the third time.

'It's up here somewhere.' He gave her an equally bitter look in return. 'And you could get out and help me look next time.'

'Could I?' she snarled back, slamming the car into gear. 'Maybe you could read your map more carefully *next time*.'

'It's here somewhere, dammit!'

'I won't hold my breath.'

They drove on for three or four minutes, then Belinda slammed on the brakes yet again. Ignoring Howard, she opened the car door, slid out and set off across the rough ground.

Howard opened his too, and yelled at her over the car top.

'What have you stopped for now?'

'It might be here.'

'Are you blind, woman? This is nothing like it!'

'And I suppose you were absolutely right when you picked the last place and the one before?'

'At least I've been there before!'

'You don't have to shout at me because I haven't!'

'You shouted at me first!'

'I did not! Even at breakfast you were shouting at me!'

'For heaven's sake! You clear off and pick up another man, leave me twiddling my thumbs at the hotel, don't bother to apologise afterwards, and then you shout at me for shouting at you!'

'I did not pick up another man!'

'Don't tell me Gunther doesn't rate as a man!'

'He's a damn sight more of one than you are! At least he has feelings, while you're chillier than a lump of frozen haddock!'

'You don't have the slightest idea what goes on inside my head!'

'Your head?' She took a couple of steps back towards the car, and glared at him over the roof. 'I sometimes think that's the only organ you possess! Just because you're at the University, you think you know it all! Well, I can tell you, Howard Henderson, your head may be stuffed full of every fact under the sun, but you still don't know the first thing about women and love!'

'You didn't think that when we first came here!'

'Love? You call that love? That wasn't love, Howard, not for you! That was sex, pure and simple!'

'Was it ever!' Howard spat.

He pushed himself angrily away from the car roof, and strode purposefully around the bonnet towards her. For a moment Belinda was too agitated to move. Then it came into her head that she ought to run, but she didn't want to run, she wanted to fight! She ran at him, fists flailing, feet slipping on the rough ground.

He had her by the shoulders, and her punches were railing ineffectually on the broad expanse of his chest. And then he was pulling her closer, and she had no room to hit him any more.

His mouth descended on hers with punishing force, driving her lips bruisingly apart. Involuntarily her arms moved around her shoulders, and he moved to mould her body close to his.

'Forgotten what we had?' he growled at her. 'Forgotten what it really was? Well, let me just remind you!'

He *was* reminding her. Her body seemed to respond to his like a desert after rain. Passion flowered inside her at every touch of his hands, his lips, his body.

She was as frantic as he now, not with temper but with intense desire. Whatever he felt, whatever he was offering her, she wanted it! Her body moved urgently, restlessly against his, taking and offering at the same time.

'Come a bit further from the road,' Howard murmured, freeing his mouth momentarily from its exploration of her neck and collarbone.

'Howard, we——'

'Nobody will come.' He drew away, still holding one of her hands, and led her, more gently now, down the slope till they were out of sight of the road. They passed behind a clump of bushes, and slid down together on to the short, rough, flower-strewn grass.

'Oh, yes!' Belinda didn't want to think, simply to feel.

And every feeling, everything in her mind, was of Howard: the taste, the touch, the smell of him. He was pulling off the flimsy scraps of her sunsuit, struggling with the fastening of his shorts. She reached up to help him, and then they were free of their clothing, and he was moving to take her, and the world expanded to infinity and contracted to a pinprick of unbelievable intensity.

Her desires had been as dammed-up as she had accused his of being, and it was with the intense relief of a balloon bursting, a river breaking its banks, that they flooded out in the ecstatic release of their union. Then she was slowly, slowly coming to her senses; oddly and acutely aware of the bright blueness of the sky, the relentless heat of the sun, the warm sweet smell of the spring plants crushed beneath them.

And the unbearable realisation that she had given in to him again—and won not the tiniest of concessions in return.

CHAPTER EIGHT

'WE CAN'T stay here,' Howard said quietly. 'Come on.'

No, they couldn't. It was neither the smoothest nor the most private of beds. But Belinda would have laughed off the thistles and the ants, even the faint risk that a car might come along the track, if only she'd felt joy at what had happened.

But how could she? Oh, she had wanted him badly, and her physical pleasure had been intense. But she hadn't meant to make love to him again on his terms, and it was with a low feeling of self-disgust that she followed him back to the car.

'Thirsty?' Howard asked. 'There's some water in the hamper, isn't there?'

There was. He unscrewed the top of the bottle and handed a cupful to her. Without looking at him, she accepted it and drank.

'Lindy,' Howard said softly.

'We'd better forget that happened,' she responded in an unsteady voice.

'No, we will not!' Firmly, he took the plastic cup out of her hands and tossed it on to the ground. His hands, descending on her shoulders, pulled her round to face him.

'We can't go on as we have been doing,' he growled. 'It's been killing both of us. All right, you wish I were different in some ways, and I think the same of you. But what we've got is so good. I've never known anything like it before, and nor have you, have you?'

'But it's not right! You just don't feel——'

'Right now I feel plenty!' His hands dug into the soft flesh of her shoulders, forcing her to submit and listen to him. 'I know I'm not good at sloppy words, but I do care about you in my way. I care a lot. You know that really, don't you?'

'Maybe I do,' she whispered.

'We've both been stupid. It's true, I'm scared of my feelings. I know I've been busy digging out my defences when I could have been negotiating with you. I know I've been secretive, and you've found that hard to bear. But we can try to change that, can't we?'

'Can we?'

'If that's what we both want. And I thought it was. . .?'

Belinda shook her head. 'I just can't think straight right now.'

'Then don't. Don't think. Just hold me for a while.'

She did. She moved closer into his arms, and let hers slide around the warm bulk of his body. She could feel his heart thumping through his thin shirt. And her own, answering it, its rhythm slowly settling into contentment.

He was right. Wasn't he? He wasn't just looking for sex any more, he *did* care about her, and he had shown it in dozens of ways, large and small, over the previous few weeks. Perhaps it really was time for them to abandon their battle lines, call a truce, and try to find out whether the gulf between them really was as great as they had come to imagine it to be?

If Howard would try, really try, to open himself out to her, wouldn't that give them room to try to develop the kind of relationship she was looking for? Wasn't it worth a try at least? She wanted him so badly, and in his way he seemed to want her too.

'OK?' he asked in a low voice.

'I think so. If you'll talk to me, really talk, then——'

'Then we could make it work?'

'Maybe we could.' She eased her grip on him, slowly loosening their embrace till she could move a step away. 'But I do mean really talk, Howard. Starting now.'

'But I was all set to carry on looking for the site,' Howard moaned—but with a smile that assured her he didn't really mean it.

They unloaded their belongings from the car, and Howard moved it off the road while Belinda found a comparatively smooth patch of ground not too far away. They spread out their beachmats, oiled their exposed skin, and settled down side by side under the hot sun.

'Nervous?' Belinda asked.

'A bit.'

'No need to be. I'm not the dentist!'

'No, but——' Howard paused, and a frown slid across his face. It wasn't a rejecting frown, it was a worried one, as if she was asking something impossibly hard of him, and he wasn't confident of being able to provide it.

'But what?'

'Oh, never mind.'

But I do mind, Belinda thought silently. It seemed extraordinary to her that the prospect of chatting to his lover should make Howard so tense and uncertain.

Hadn't he made that clear, though, from the start? He wasn't used to confiding in anyone. He was a brilliantly clever man in his own field, but when it came to communicating on an emotional level he might still be back in the kindergarten!

'It's not so difficult,' she whispered, and reached out a hand to touch his cheek.

'Talking to you? I know.' He gave her a rueful smile.

'Even babies do it. But it's never going to come as easily to me as it does to you.'

'That's OK, so long as you really try.'

'So where do I start?'

'I don't know! Let's say—start by telling me about your girlfriend, the one who got married.'

'Deirdre? But there's nothing to tell you.'

'Oh, yes, there is! Come on, Howard. Really try.'

'Well, she was—I mean she is, but she was to me— middling height, a little taller than you. She had dark hair, cut straight, fairly long, and brown eyes.'

'Yes, but what was she *like?*'

'She works at the University, of course: she's a mathematician.'

'Quiet?'

'Rather quiet, yes. She's a serious sort of person—she doesn't giggle like you, and she dresses much more soberly.'

'Was it love at first sight?'

'Was it *what?*'

His expression made her laugh. 'All right,' she amended cheerfully, 'did you fancy her right away?'

'I suppose I must have done. She's pretty, and she has a good figure, and I do like women!'

'I've noticed. So how often did you see her?'

'Not all that much. I was often away on field trips, and she went to the occasional conference too. When we were both in Melchester I suppose we'd meet up about once a week. We'd go to the cinema or the theatre, or eat out.'

'Once a week! Is that all?'

'It wasn't such a big deal,' Howard said defensively. 'We're both busy people, both wrapped up in our work, and that suited us fine.'

'Until she met this other man and married him.'

'Yes, well, that came as a surprise.'

'Why, were you happy? Did you think she was happy?'

'I suppose so. She never said she wasn't. We never had arguments about our relationship.'

'What did you talk about?'

'Work, mainly. I'm no mathematician and she's no botanist, but we always used to follow each other's work pretty carefully.'

'I know: secretly you love to have somebody tell you you're doing wonderfully.'

'Oh, no, Deirdre was never like that! She was much more rigorous. She'd listen to my plans and then point out the weaknesses, read my work over and check the grammar and spelling. She was very good on that kind of thing, very helpful.'

'Sounds a bit depressing to me.'

'I thought it was admirable of her.'

'In a way, yes, but I can't imagine I'd like it if a boyfriend of mine criticised my work. I don't mind if my workmates do that, but from boyfriends and my mum and dad I like to have praise!'

'I'd better give you some, then. I think you're a beautiful woman and a wonderful secretary too. Will that do?'

'And I think you're a marvellous botanist, and the best lover in the world.'

He laughed out loud, and Belinda laughed too—but she also reached out and hugged him, to assure him that she meant it.

Imagine not being used to loving words! she thought with astonishment. Imagine seeing somebody for years, and always getting cool criticism from them! How could he have endured it for so long? She certainly couldn't have done. She would certainly change that aspect of his life—and fast.

'It's funny,' Howard said thoughtfully, 'but I'd sometimes go to parties, or out in a group with Deirdre, and I'd hear other men say that kind of thing to her. I just never thought of doing it myself. Then when she told me she was marrying Professor Thorne, I couldn't help wondering whether I'd done something wrong.'

'You didn't love her, that's what was wrong.'

'That was part of it. I never wanted her desperately, in the way I want you. I never got jealous when other men chatted her up, the way I felt when you told me you'd had supper with Gunther. But even so I might have sent her Valentine cards and all that junk, and I never did.'

'No chocolates? No flowers? No surprise outings?'

'I didn't think people really did that sort of thing.'

'I bet Professor Thorne does!'

'I guess I'll have to do it this time around, if I'm to hold the competition at bay.'

'Not for that reason,' Belinda said softly. 'There isn't any competition, Howard. Oh, lots of men sniff around, they always have, but it's you I love and nobody else. I don't need all that to keep me from straying—but I would like it anyway!'

'Than you shall have it.' His kiss, firm and confident, reassured her of that.

'And so shall you. You'll be amazed to find out what fun it is!'

Their laughter faded as their kisses intensified: but not into lovemaking this time, just into a close, warm embrace. Belinda rested her head on Howard's shoulder. 'I could just go to sleep in the sun,' she murmured.

'Do.'

And she did.

Late in the afternoon they made another attempt to find Howard's lost site, and to their relief they discovered it quite quickly. The markers were badly overgrown, but once they'd found one of them they soon tracked down the rest, and set about roping the site off so they would find it more easily the next day.

They didn't do any more substantial work. It was enough to be together, to enjoy the sun and each other, to talk a little and laugh a little and make love again, this time on a more carefully chosen and secluded patch of ground.

It was late when they got back to the hotel at Rethimnon, though not too late: Belinda had insisted that she wanted to swim, and Howard had agreed to join her. They took a brief and invigorating dip together in the cold water, then went back to change before going out to eat.

'Now what should I wear?' Belinda mused out loud. Howard, newly showered, damp and happy, was lounging on her bed, and the contents of her suitcase were—as usual—strewn all over it.

'Show me that white dress. I haven't seen that before, have I?'

'This one?' She picked up a simple cotton dress which had been folded at the bottom of the case. 'I did wear it once in Sitia, I think. With a red belt, and my Indian bangles.'

'Wear it this time without them,' Howard instructed.

'Without any of them? I can't do that!'

'Put it on and let me see.'

Belinda slipped it over her head.

'No, it needs the belt. Yes, just like that. That's fine.'

'It needs *some* jewellery too.'

'No, it doesn't. You make yourself look too fussy.'

'I don't!' She caught a glimpse of his expression, and amended that. 'Oh, all right, I do a little. Mum and Charmian get at me all the time for piling on too much, but I just enjoy doing it. I like looking good and having people look at me. That's what you don't like, isn't it? You want to fade into the background, and I don't!'

'Darling, you could never do that.' Howard got up from the bed and caught her in a hug that lifted her feet right off the floor. 'No, I don't want that. I don't want to tone you down into a grey person, and I don't mind other men admiring you, so long as you're mine! But I do wish you'd try to look a little more grown-up.'

And *I* wish you'd love me as I am, Belinda thought to herself. She didn't criticise Howard's clothes, even when she privately thought they were boring: why should he criticise hers? But somehow it seemed that this was important to him, and she let him lead her to the mirror and take a look in it.

'See?' he said. 'It's fine like that.'

'I suppose I do,' she conceded, rather grumpily. 'Oh, men! Good taste!'

'I'd let you choose what I wore too, but I warn you all I have with me is jeans, jeans or jeans! I'll take you out to dinner in a suit when we get back to England, though.'

'I'll hold you to that,' she retorted—and turned her head round, pulling him to her for a kiss. 'Now come on, I'm starving!'

For the first time, Belinda woke up the next morning with Howard at her side. She had insisted that he stay

the night instead of retreating to his room, and after a
brief argument they had agreed to sleep together in his
much tidier room.

She was awake for a few moments before he stirred:
time to lie and gaze at him, his arms flung apart, the
sheet tangled across him, halfway down his bare muscular torso, his face softened in repose.

How magnificent he was! And how tigerish he could
be too, when something didn't suit him. Fancy caring so
much about a few clothes strewn across the floor! But
she sensed that in some inexplicable way her untidiness
really did matter to him, and that made it matter to her.

It wasn't only he who would have to change if their
relationship were to flourish, she acknowledged to herself. While he worked on opening up to her, she would
have to work on dressing more subtly and keeping things
tidy to please him.

It wouldn't be easy. But it would be worth it, surely,
if her reward was to still Howard's last doubts, and to
win a lasting commitment from him.

He stirred, murmuring something half under his
breath. She reached out her hand to touch his cheek
softly. Then his eyes flickered open, and she moved
closer, snuggling down by his side, feeling the warmth of
him next to her.

It soon turned into the usual hardworking kind of day:
Howard wasn't the man to let passion get in the way of
his life's work for long. But there was a relaxed and
happy mood around them that made Belinda even more
sorry they had wasted so much of their time on Crete in
silly squabbles.

Howard contented was like a different man. His smile
added an extra dimension of charm to his handsome
features. He talked to her on the journey to the site,

easily and openly, not about intimate matters but about botany, politics, the people they had met and a dozen other subjects. And when she chattered away he responded with evident interest and pleasure, even laughing out loud once or twice.

When they got down to work he became more serious, but still there was an infectious enthusiasm about him.

How good it was, working with him! They seemed to work really well together. Even when they had been arguing the work had gone reasonably smoothly, but now it went marvellously, as if they had an instinctive understanding on every level.

The more Belinda saw of Howard at work, the more she admired him. He was methodical, but never plodding. His knowledge astonished her. He was a thoughtful boss, too, taking care to keep her informed and to delegate a little responsibility to her.

She felt privileged to help with his research. And if her own talents were less exceptional, she felt sure she was doing a good job as his assistant. Whatever the state of her hotel room, all the notes she took were neat and tidy. Though she was hardly a botanist on Howard's level, she had taken a real interest in the work from the start, and now she could recognise most of the plants before he named them to her.

They ate a simple lunch sitting in the sun, and made love afterwards in the open air. Their lovemaking had always been good, but now it seemed even better, more tender without losing any of its excitement.

Belinda was lying in Howard's arms, warm and sated in the midday sun, when she noticed a purple flowering plant growing in a clump of tall grass a few feet away from them.

'That looks like a new one,' she said dreamily.

'That what?'

'That flower. It's pretty. It's a pity we can't pick them. Photos are all very well, but sometimes I'd really like to go back to a hotel room full of smells like these.'

'That's the first rule, never to pick the flowers.'

'I do know that, darling! What is it, anyway?'

'Show me.'

Belinda rolled over, sat up, and searched again for it. 'Over here.'

Howard stretched, stood up, and made his way to where she was indicating. He bent down and parted the grass.

'Fancy that! It looks almost like. . .' Gently, he pushed the grass down so that he could see it better.

'It's a kind of orchid, isn't it?'

'A kind, certainly. . . I thought for a moment it was an *Orchis Anatolica*—an Anatolian Orchid—but there's something about the formation of the flower lip. . .' He looked up again, dawning excitement on his face. 'You know, this looks to be an extremely rare hybrid variety.'

'A rare one? Oh, how exciting! Are you going to take lots of photos of it?'

'Of course I am. I rather think it's the first of this particular sub-species I've ever seen.'

'That's marvellous!'

'Sure is. It's an exceptional discovery. Belinda, you're a marvel! This really makes my day.'

'I thought I'd already done that for you!'

'All of it makes my day! You and the plant and—well, life altogether!'

Howard's beaming expression, as he straightened up, echoed all the enthusiasm of his words. Belinda, rising too, reached out impulsively to give him a big hug.

'Come on then, botanist, get your camera!'

'You stay here.' He deposited a quick kiss on her mouth. 'Don't let me lose it.'

'It's not going anywhere,' she called out, laughing, as Howard hurried back to the car.

Moments later he was back with his cameras and accessories. The rare orchid demanded especial care, and he took it, judging his angles and exposure meticulously, though without losing any of his infectious enthusiasm. Indeed, it had grown on him, until he was like an archaeologist unearthing gold, or an art lover finding an unknown Rembrandt in a country auction.

'Champagne tonight,' he crowed, as he finally stowed away his cameras. 'But we haven't finished work yet. We'll have to check over the rest of this area, just in case there are more examples.'

'Howard, this isn't even part of our site!'

'But for a hybrid Anatolian Orchid, darling. . .'

'A botanist will do anything,' she finished with a laugh. 'OK, boss. You tell me where to search and I'll get to it!'

The remainder of their time in Crete seemed to fly past. Their understanding with each other seemed firm now, and rather than agonise still more over their relationship they were both happy to let it develop at its own pace.

As it did, steadily. They worked hard all day, relaxed together in the evenings, and spent nights together filled with joy and passion. They sunbathed and swam and drank thick red wine, and at the weekend they drifted round the towns and villages and tourist attractions to the west of the island.

It was a sorrow to them both when they came to the last day of work on Howard's final wild flower site. They logged the last anemone, the last orchid, then disentangled the rope from Howard's markers and left the site—with luck, to remain untouched for another five years.

They had agreed to have a special supper to mark the end of the trip, and Belinda retreated to her own room at the hotel to change into one of her prettiest outfits: a citrus yellow sundress patterned with palm trees and orange sunbursts.

Maybe it was a little more garish than Howard would approve, she thought ruefully, arranging a handful of gold chains around her neck, then reluctantly discarding them again. Just a red belt; her red espadrilles to match; her hair brushed into relative tameness—and that looked like a good foil for his sobriety, didn't it?

Of course it did. This wasn't England, and she wasn't going to dress as she had at Cornwell Electronics, not even for Howard. He'd see that she had at least made some effort to confirm to his preferences, and once they were home she would continue to work on pleasing him.

He was waiting for her in the hotel bar.

'I'm not late, am I?' she asked, joining him at the counter and taking his arm.

'No, it's only——' a quick check of his watch '—thirty-seven minutes since we got back. Must be a record!'

'I didn't want to waste any of our last evening here together.'

'Absolutely not, though there'll be many more evenings, I hope, when we're back in England. Gin and tonic?'

'Orange juice,' she corrected him. 'This'll be our last night, though—at least, until the next field trip. Think of that!'

'I don't think I want to,' Howard rejoined lightly.

He caught the barman's eye and ordered their drinks. They sat at a small table by the window, overlooking the blue expanse of the Mediterranean.

No, Belinda didn't want to think of that either, but she couldn't help being aware of it, and feeling a sense of sorrow. It wouldn't do to mar their last night by dwelling too much on what would follow it, but she knew that things wouldn't be quite the same in England. Of course they would carry on seeing each other—there was no real doubt of that, when things were so good between them—but in future their lovemaking would be a matter of snatched hours and half-hours, not of long lazy nights together. At least, it would be like that at first, though perhaps later she could hope for. . .

'What are you thinking?' Howard asked softly.

'Oh, about England.' She smiled, a little wryly. 'It'll be good to see Mum and Dad and Charmian again, but I'll miss waking up with you in the mornings.'

'You'll have to stay over at my house sometimes. Then you won't miss it.'

'Oh, I couldn't do that!'

She said it automatically, without forethought, but without thinking, either, that he could conceivably disagree. But from his slight frown, and the way he leaned forward, it was immediately evident that she had been mistaken.

'Why not?'

'It wouldn't be right. I mean, I just couldn't.'

'You've spent the night with me here, lots of times. Why should it be any less right in England?'

'Because of my family, of course! They'll like you, I'm sure, and of course you'll be welcome at any time round at our house. But your welcome won't stretch to an overnight stay, I'm afraid—and if I were to stay out overnight myself Mum would have a heart attack!'

'Perhaps it won't be such a good idea for you to live with your parents, then.'

'But I'll enjoy it, on the whole. Anyway, though they didn't mind me sharing a flat in London, I'm sure they'd be terribly hurt if I moved out to live somewhere else in Melchester. Until I get married, of course.'

'I dare say they'd get used to it.'

But I don't want them to get used to it. That was what Belinda thought—but she hesitated before saying it, and then decided not to.

She could see what Howard had in mind. Herself living in a flat just round the corner from him, maybe sharing with a couple of other University secretaries, keeping her mess to herself there, and calling round to spend the evening—and the night—with him a couple of times a week. Or more.

She could have done it, too. Jennifer and Graham would have grumbled. They would probably have guessed her motives and been scathing about them, but they wouldn't have disowned her or done anything dramatic. They trusted her to run her own life.

But that wasn't really what she wanted. What she wanted was marriage to Howard. She felt sure of that now. She was in love with him, committed to their relationship, and she wanted to set the seal of permanency on it.

She knew he loved her too. But he'd been so hesitant in making his own commitments that she didn't dare to take it for granted that he'd propose to her in the near future. He needed to be nudged in the right direction. And she'd nudge him much more effectively if she frustrated him by returning to Jennifer and Graham every night than if she spent nights with him, and made him *too* content with their unmarried state!

'I don't think it would be fair to them, though,' she said instead, in a casual way that put an end to the conversation. And she made sure of that by drawing Howard's attention to a fishing-boat a little way out at sea, and persuading him to talk about the scenery in front of them.

CHAPTER NINE

'COME to supper with us tonight,' Belinda urged, once they were clear of Customs and driving back to Melchester. 'It's six now, so we should be home just before seven. I don't know what Mum's cooking, but she can usually stretch it to one more.'

'I wouldn't do that,' said Howard.

'Why not? You don't have any other plans, do you?'

'No, but I'd be imposing. Your parents don't know me, and they'll want to hear all about the trip from you.'

'They'll hear it all!' She grinned at him. 'But they won't mind hearing about it from you as well.'

'Maybe, but I'd rather not.'

'You wouldn't be imposing, honestly. They don't think like that. You're my boyfriend, Howard. They know that, they know I want to be with you, and they're curious to meet you. I don't like to think of you going back to an empty house and cooking a couple of sausages from the freezer, while I get Mum's best stew and all the family to tell everything to. It isn't fair.'

'Belinda, I do choose to live alone.'

'You can't like it, though!'

'Why not?'

Temporarily, Belinda was silenced. *Why not*? Wasn't it obvious? No flatmates, no sister to argue with, no parents to cheer you up, nothing but you and the television and four blank walls? She'd have gone mad in a week!

But she knew Howard had lived on his own for ten years now, ever since he had graduated. He was used to it. They weren't similar in temperament, and she had more sense than to assume that he always responded exactly as she would do. Just because she'd have detested going back to an empty house, it didn't mean that he mightn't find it enjoyable to have at least some time on his own.

Perhaps he even felt ready for time like that just then. During the month in Crete they had scarcely been apart. If he wasn't used to living with someone, then he must have found it strange to have her around all the time. He might welcome a little peace and quiet, without her Madonna records or her constant chatter.

Or he might believe he would, she went on to think— and find himself mistaken! Leaving her to the warm welcome of her family, then driving home alone to a cold house, might bring it home to him how good it would be to get married to her, and build a warm household of his own.

'Come tomorrw, then,' she said.

'You'd better check with your parents first.'

'There's no need; they're always happy to have company. But since it's you, I'll warn them.'

'Do that. I'll phone you tomorrow morning, OK?'

They were already turning into her street. She could see her parents' house, with the hall and living-room lights sending a warm glow out across the road. Soon she'd be tumbling out of the car, and hugging all her family as they welcomed her back.

And Howard would be going home to sleep alone.

'Do that,' she agreed quietly.

'There's something for you in the conservatory!' Jennifer called out, as Belinda let herself in after work, four days later.

'In the conservatory?'

'Go and see.'

She did. There, lying on the wicker table, was a vast bouquet of flowers.

'Oh, Mum!'

'They're beautiful, aren't they?' Jennifer agreed, following her in. 'They only arrived an hour ago, just after Charmian got home from school, so I reckoned they could survive without water until you came home.'

Belinda was barely listening—she was too busy gazing at the bouquet. They were fragile late spring and summer flowers, irises and gladioli and asters. Just the kind of flowers she and Howard had been working with on Crete.

She didn't really need to look at the card that came with the bouquet in order to know who it came from. But it was a joy to read it anyway.

A little reminder for you—you said you'd love to have the same scents at home. Love, Howard.

'Oh, isn't that lovely, Mum?'

'You hardly need me to tell you it is,' Jennifer teased. 'Now, if you can bear to unwrap the cellophane, you'd better put them in water.'

'I'll have to thank him this evening,' Belinda ruminated, as she retraced her steps to the kitchen.

'You're going over to his house again tonight?' asked her mother.

'After supper, yes. That's OK, isn't it, Mum?'

'It's up to you, love. But I do hope you're going to bring Howard round to meet us some time soon. . .?'

'I will,' Belinda assured her—but without glancing round from the bouquet, which she was busily dismantling. She'd been to Howard's house every night since coming home. And each time she'd asked him to come round to the Barfords' for supper; and each time he'd casually but firmly refused. He always had an excuse for turning down the invitations. Anyway, they could make love at his house, he'd pointed out, and they could hardly do that at hers. Which was true, but she wanted him to meet Jennifer and Graham and Charmian, and they wanted to meet him, and his reluctance to come was an irritant to her happiness.

But she couldn't have felt angry with him right then, and it was with a light heart that she assured herself that she'd repeat the invitation, more insistently, that evening.

Nipping into the common-room at the Plant Research Unit for a cup of coffee at eleven one morning the following week, Belinda saw Howard sitting in the corner, talking earnestly to Peter Miller, one of the other researchers.

She half raised her hand in greeting; closeted with the photocopier all morning, she had scarcely seen him. But he gave her the barest glance before turning back to his conversation.

And when she had obtained her coffee and was looking for a seat he didn't glance up again and gesture to her to come over.

'Joining me, Belinda?'

'Oh, sure, Sarah.' With a smile, she followed Sarah, another of the Unit's secretaries, to another corner of the room. And she had a pleasant chat with her about the Unit's work and its personalities, but still it grated on her a little that Howard was paying her no attention at all.

Half watching him as she chatted, she saw him drain

the last of his coffee, and rise to his feet. He lingered, standing with his back to her, saying goodbye to Peter, then without another glance in her direction he strode out of the room.

'Belinda? Belinda, did you hear me?'

'What? Oh, sorry, Sarah, I was miles away.'

'I asked if you were free on Friday, to come ten-pin bowling with us. There's a whole group of staff from the Unit who go regularly.'

'This Friday? It should be all right, but I ought to check with Howard.'

'Howard? That's your boyfriend?'

'That's right. It's just possible he's got something planned for us already.'

'Well, you can let me know any time this week.' Sarah smiled. 'That must be funny, you know—having a boyfriend with the same name as your boss.'

Belinda smiled back, but she could feel the effort in her face muscles. 'Actually they're the same man. I thought you knew I was going out with Howard Henderson?'

'Oh. Sorry, I hope I didn't make too much of a boob there. I honestly hadn't realised. You know, Howard's such a loner, and I rather assumed you and he were just. . .'

'Just boss and secretary?' Belinda finished for her. 'Well, no, we are a little more than that.'

'Lucky you,' Sarah said easily. 'Bring him along too if you can.'

'I'll ask him,' Belinda assured her. 'Now I really ought to be getting back to work.'

She retraced her steps up the stairs and along the corridor. She passed Howard's room before she reached her own, and paused outside the door. Should she call in now and say something to him?

Perhaps she should. A little hurt was festering inside her, and she knew it might keep her from concentrating on her work. But his door was firmly closed, and in the end she decided it would be better to wait until she saw him that evening, and talk to him properly then.

'So the dog sat outside the rabbit hole waiting. He waited until it got dark, and then the rabbits sneaked out of a different hole and round the back of him, and one of them tweaked at his tail. The dog turned round, but he couldn't see them, so he called out, "Why did you do that?" And one of the rabbits called back to him, "It's a shaggy dog tail!"'

Belinda spluttered and groaned. 'Dad, that's appalling!'

'Shaggy dog tail. Shaggy dog tale. Get it?'

'But it's got nothing to do with the. . .'

'That's why it's so funny!'

'Graham, it's a terrible joke,' Jennifer assured him, though her laughter belied her words as she rose to clear the soup plates from the table.

'You tell a better one, then. Howard, you tell a better one.'

'I won't promise it's better, but have you heard the one about the two Irishmen in New York?'

'The one where they go up the Empire State Building?'

'No, in this one they go to look at the Statue of Liberty. And. . .'

Belinda reached for the wine bottle, and refilled her glass. She refilled her father's too, and Howard's on the other side of her. They had all been drinking, but not heavily: no need to, when they had been in fits of laughter ever since supper started.

Howard telling a joke! She'd never have believed it. He did it well too, piling on the irrelevancies and pacing himself carefully. He arrived at the punchline just as Jennifer and Charmian reappeared with risotto and salad. He paused for a moment while they set down the dishes, then carried on to finish the story.

Graham laughed loudly, and Charmian's new boy-friend Giles did too—and so did Belinda.

Her eyes had been on Howard all the time. He seemed quite different now from the remote man who had failed to notice her that morning.

It pleased her to see how much he was at home at her parents' house. This was the second time he'd come to the Barfords' for supper, and, in spite of all his hesitations, he'd taken only minutes to settle in. He wasn't lurking anonymously in the background, either: he'd joined in enthusiastically with every topic of conversation.

She knew he hadn't wanted to come initially, and when she'd pushed him he had still protested that he'd hate it. But if this was hating it, she was a damp haddock! This was Howard as she had always believed he could be, open and relaxed and giving.

Graham was embarked on yet another bad joke, Howard was leaning forward to hear it, and Jennifer, ladling risotto on to a pile of warmed plates, caught Belinda's eye and winked at her.

It's working, that wink said. And it looked as if it was. But underneath Belinda's pleasure, the morning's hurt niggled—and the awareness that this wasn't the moment to bring it up.

* * *

Supper went on till past nine-thirty, with much cheerful argument being pursued over the table. Then the family retreated to the living-room to argue about which television programmes they'd watch, and which video for later. Howard settled on the sofa and slipped an arm round Belinda when she squeezed in next to him. Charmian insisted on watching a glitzy mini-series and he watched it with them. It wasn't his cup of tea, Belinda knew, but at least he didn't complain out loud that it was sentimental rubbish.

He didn't stir during the news, and it was only when Graham rose, stretched and announced that he had to be up early in the morning that he reluctantly got to his feet.

'Come again tomorrow,' Jennifer suggested. 'It's Belinda's night to do supper for us. What's it to be, Lindy—your best lasagne?'

'If you'll come I'll do that,' said Belinda.

'I wish I could—but there's a departmental meeting after work tomorrow.'

'Then come round when it finishes,' Jennifer urged.

'I can't ask you to hold supper for me—it might go on for hours. Can I invite myself on Thursday instead?'

'You don't need to invite youself,' Graham assured him. 'You're welcome any time.'

'That's so kind.'

'It's pure self-interest,' Belinda said with a smile. 'I'd make their lives a misery if you didn't come! I won't be long, Mum.'

'I've got better things to do than to stand at the door waiting for you, love!'

The sound of the family's laughter followed them as they closed the front door behind them, and moved towards each other in the small enclosed space of the porch.

A kiss—or rather, several kisses, though they served only to inflame their desire, not to quench it.

'Mmm,' Howard murmured. 'I wish you could come home with me.'

'I wish you could come back round tomorrow,' she shot back.

'That's hardly the same.' He drew her still closer, moulding her buttocks with his hands and pressing her to him so that she was fully aware of the intensity of his arousal. 'You know what I want, and I can't have it while your family are all around us.'

'So do I, darling. You won't be very late tomorrow, will you? Why don't you phone me when you get back home, and I'll come round then?'

'Yes, do that.' One last lingering kiss, and they reluctantly eased their grip on each other. Belinda stood watching as Howard shrugged his jacket up around his neck, and set off into the chill drizzle of the spring evening.

She could have said something then. No, she couldn't really: it might have led an enjoyable evening to end on a sour note. The next evening, when they were alone in Howard's house, would give her a much better opportunity.

'That's. . .much. . .better.' With kisses punctuating each word, Howard slowly eased himself off his bed, and went to fetch the coffee that he had poured earlier. He brought back both cups, his and Belinda's, set them on the bedside table, and slid back under the covers next to her.

Belinda felt her muscles contract as her arms instinctively prepared to move out towards him. But she held them back.

Perhaps she shouldn't have made love with him before they talked, but she'd wanted it so much, and so had he. And it had been good—but not that good. All the time, she'd been conscious of her nagging uncertainty.

It had happened again that day. A postgraduate student had called into Howard's room when she was there going over a chapter of the book with him, and he hadn't bothered to introduce her. All right, the student had taken it for granted that Belinda was Howard's secretary—but she and Howard were clearly on friendly terms, and Belinda would have liked to be introduced properly, and as *more* than his secretary. At the Plant Research Unit, though, he never, but never, made her feel like anything more.

He was different at her parents' house, admittedly. He was different when they were alone together. But why did he have to switch off his emotions so completely when they were in the company of his colleagues? A little bit of affection between them surely wouldn't have been taken amiss.

He smiled at her, a lazily contented, satiated smile. And Belinda smiled back, a little nervously.

'We've got an invitation for this Friday,' she said.

'Oh?'

'To go bowling. Apparently there's a group from the Unit who go every week. I don't know if you've been before?'

'No, I haven't.'

'Like to come this time?'

'I can't, I'm afraid. I'll be going up to Bradford to see my parents.'

'Oh.' A pause. 'Can I come with you?'

'I'd rather you didn't.'

'Well, I'd rather I did.'

She sensed, rather than felt, him stiffen next to her. 'Belinda, I said no.'

'But I'd like to meet your parents,' she insisted. 'You've met my family, and I've got to meet yours some time.'

'I don't think that's necessary.'

'Don't think that's necessary!' She sat up in bed, covers slipping off her, her face pink with hurt and confusion. 'But, Howard, they're your *parents*.'

'You wouldn't enjoy meeting them.'

'It's not a matter of enjoying it! Though I bet I would. It's a question of——' Her voice caught on a sob. 'Sometimes I feel as if you're ashamed of me,' she finished unsteadily.

'That's ridiculous.'

'No, it's not! I've known since we came back that there was something wrong, and I'm sure now that that's it. At the Unit, too, you don't show me off to people; you don't tell them about us.'

'But that's work.'

'It's not only work. At least, it isn't as if work and family and me are little compartments in your life that you have to keep separate. They're all supposed to mesh together to make up your life. I want to be your partner in every aspect of you life. Not a sexual partner that you keep hidden away like a guilty secret, but your girlfriend, your other half.'

'Now, just a minute!' Howard exclaimed, sitting up too.

'No, you wait just a minute! It's not right, it's not fair, and I'm not putting up with it! If I'm going to be your girlfriend, then I'm not going to be treated like that. You acted in the common-room yesterday as if you didn't know me, and you weren't much better when Jane Arthur came in this morning. So what's wrong with me? What is it you're ashamed of?'

'What's wrong with you? You know that. I've told you already. You push!'

'I what?'

'You push all the time. More, more, more. Every time, the stakes for sleeping with you seem to go up. Tell me more, you said. So I'm telling you more. Now it's let me share more. Well, I don't particularly want to share more of my life with you. And if I do, next it'll be "When are we getting married?" I'll tell you now the answer to that. Never. Because I don't want more. Understand? I'm happy with things as they are now. I don't want you worming into every aspect of my life. I don't want marriage, and I don't want anything that looks like marriage. And if you can't settle for me on those terms, then it just won't work for us.'

The blood seemed to have left Belinda's body. She had gone cold, very cold. Her hands gripping the sheet were clenched into claws.

She couldn't say anything. She couldn't even frame the words, let alone bring them out.

'Oh, God,' Howard said in a defeated voice. He threw back the bedcovers and clambered out. Numbly, Belinda watched him stalk across to the chair where he had thrown his clothes earlier.

He stepped into underpants and trousers. He pulled his sweatshirt over his head. Then he turned to her.

'I told you,' he said coldly. 'I told you right from the start. I said I didn't want marriage. There's no point looking at me now as if I've conned you, because I was straight with you all along. I told you what I was offering, and you took it on those terms.'

So she had. But not really. He'd said it, and she'd heard it, but she hadn't really believed he meant it. All along she'd believed that she'd change his mind.

And she hadn't. Her efforts had failed, failed utterly. She had held out for more, and he'd given her more—but a tiny, tiny amount more compared to all that she had wanted from him.

'If you're upset now, you've only yourself to blame,' Howard continued, his voice hard and vicious.

That was true, Belinda thought dully. He'd been consistent all along. The fault was hers, for failing to listen to what he had been telling her.

She willed her hands to unclench. The sheet fell out of them. Slowly, sluggishly, oblivious of the nakedness she presented to him, she clambered out of bed.

'Belinda,' Howard said awkwardly.

She didn't answer him as she groped for her clothes.

'Don't wreck it. What we've got is good—you know that. Don't wreck it by asking for things I can't give you.'

Asking for them? She wasn't asking for them, she was aching for them, longing for them with every fibre of her being.

These were Howard's terms. She could see them now, in all their cold clarity. And for all the joy his lovemaking had brought her, she couldn't accept them.

'Lindy, I'll see you in the morning. OK?'

No, not OK. Not OK at all. With fumbling fingers Belinda pulled her clothes back on. She retrieved her shoulderbag from the floor, stepped into her shoes. She walked downstairs, conscious of Howard following a couple of paces behind her. She didn't turn round to him as she unlatched the front door of his house and let herself out of it.

'What's for supper, Mum?'

'Lasagne. You haven't forgotten, Lindy? Howard's coming round, and you said you'd cook your special for us.'

'Oh. Well. . .actually, Mum, he's not coming.'

'He's not? Oh, dear. Something up at——'Jennifer, turning from the pile of washing she was folding, caught sight of Belinda's face and revised her first guess. 'Something up between you two.'

'It's finished, Mum.'

'It's *what*? Don't be daft, Lindy. I can see when a relationship's finished, and that one isn't. Nothing like it.'

'But he——' Belinda swallowed. 'You and Graham wouldn't understand. He's so nice when he comes round here, but when we're alone, or at the Unit, he's completely different. He's got this thing about getting committed. He acts as if I don't belong to him at all.'

Jennifer raised her eyebrows. 'Have a cup of strong coffee, love, and tell me all about it.'

Belinda sat down at the kitchen table. Her shoulders drooped. She'd had a long weary day at work, when Howard had only spoken to her in snapped-out orders. She'd been hoping against hope that after sleeping on it he would have changed his mind. Fat chance of that, though!

'He's so determined not to be committed to me,' she said listlessly.

'Oh? And why's that?'

Jennifer's calm interest was what she needed. Left alone, she might have resorted to floods of tears, but how much better it was to tell all to somebody who loved her, and get sympathy and understanding in return! She found herself telling her mother the whole story: the little she knew about Howard's home and family, his affair with Deirdre, and the ups and downs of their own relationship.

'So really,' Jenifer said slowly, when she had finished, 'there are two problems, it seems to me.'

'Are there?'

'Oh, yes. Problem one: Howard hasn't had as happy a family background as you, and he's not sure that marriage is a good thing. And problem two: he's not sure that you're the girl for him.'

'But he loves me!' Belinda protested. 'He said so, Mum. You know he did.'

'I'm sure he does, love, in his way. But look at it from his side, and maybe you'll understand. You say it seems as if he doesn't want to end up like his parents, and, from what you could tell, they weren't well matched. So that's what he's scared of: marrying somebody who's not a good match for him and facing hurt afterwards. And what would outsiders make of you and Howard?'

'Well. . .he's quieter than me. More serious.'

'So he is,' Jennifer agreed. 'Not dull, far from it, but somebody who didn't know him might take him to be a bit of a dull dog. And frankly, love, somebody who didn't know you might take you to be a bit of a fluffy bimbo.'

'Mum!'

'If I'm being cruel, Lindy, it's only to be kind. You've some wonderful qualities. You have the sunniest nature I know, and you're full of enthusiasm, and *we* know you're great company. But quite honestly, your dress sense is a bit beyond the pale. There've been times in

the past, you know, when we've been out together and
I've been tempted to act as if you don't belong to me!'

'Not quite!' Belinda managed a smile, but it was a
faint one, because she did feel the force of the criticism.
'All right, you've got a point, Mum. But I have been
trying to sober up to please Howard.'

'I know you have, love. But I also know that the
image he still has of you is the one in your snaps from
Crete, all bikinis and silly sunsuits and miles too much
jewellery. It'll take a while before he realises you're
capable of looking more conventional when you try. And
you're young, remember, and not a graduate. That
doesn't help. Set against this ex-girlfriend of his, it'd be
no wonder if not only Howard but his colleagues too
took you to be a lightweight.'

'I suppose so.' Her spirits were falling still lower by
the second. 'But there's not much I can do about that.'

'Oh, I don't know,' Jennifer said airily.

'But, Mum, I can't go to university now!'

'You could still do it if you set your mind to it, love.
Mature students are commonplace these days, and
you've got the brains, you know. But to be honest, I
don't think you need to go that far. If you really make
an effort to subdue your tastes a little, and come across
to Howard and his colleagues as an intelligent, thoughtful assistant, I think in the long run that would do the
trick.'

'I'm not subduing them too far!'

'Oh, no, love. Black suits and Mahler symphonies
isn't you, and I think it's always a mistake to try and be
someone you're not. But you could dress a little more
soberly still at work, and leave the wilder outfits for the
weekends. You could let everybody else know, and not
just us at home, that you like Beethoven as well as Bros,

that you keep up with current affairs, that you care about the state of the world.'

'Which I do.'

'Well, show it, love. Emphasise it a bit more. It seems to me that Howard is maybe supersensitive about the possibility of you showing him up, making him embarrassed, in much the same way as his mother may have been embarrassed by his father. So you need to go out of your way to show him that you can cut the ice with his friends and colleagues, and be a real credit to him.'

'You think I could?'

'Oh, yes, love. You're right, I'm sure. He does love you—it's just that he needs reassurance that you're the right person for him, and that he's not going to repeat all his parents' mistakes in reverse. And you can go one further than that, you know.'

'Can I?'

'Definitely you can. You can show him that you've got something unique to contribute to your partnership.'

'But, Mum, I'm not as clever as Howard. However hard I studied, I couldn't do as well as he's done.'

'That's true, love. But then he'll never be able to get on with people quite as easily as you do, will he?'

'True, but——'

'True, *and*,' Jennifer corrected her firmly, 'that's an invaluable skill in just about any path of life, love. I can tell you, Howard will go much further in his career, and get much more out of his life, if he marries you, than he will if he stays a bachelor. If you can only make him see it, the two of you could really complement each other just about ideally.'

'Could we?' Belinda whispered.

'I'm sure of it, love.'

CHAPTER TEN

'CHAPTER Seventeen,' Belinda announced, putting the same on Howard's desk.

'Oh. Thanks.'

'We're nearly there,' she added.

'So we are.'

He wasn't looking at her; he was scowling. His face had the tense, weary look it always seemed to have these days—ever since their argument and break-up. It had affected him deeply, Belinda knew. And every time she saw him she had a longing to wrap her arms around him and hug him and tell him that she still loved him and it was all right really, but she'd decided on her plan, a plan that certainly didn't involve behaving like that right now, and she was sticking to it.

'What does Professor Watson make of it?' she asked instead.

'Watson? Haven't shown it to him yet.'

'Haven't you? Why not?'

'Oh, he'll be too busy, at least until the end of term,' Howard said offhandedly.

'You ought to hand it over at least. If you tell him how important it is to you, I'm sure he'll have a flick through.'

'You don't know Watson, or you wouldn't say that!'

Actually I do, Belinda thought silently. Actually, darling, I'm coming to know him better than you know him yourself. But she wasn't going to say that to him straight out: she needed him to discover it for himself.

'Look,' he said impatiently, 'I've made some small revisions to Chapters Five and Six. I'll hand those over now, and leave you to put them on the word processor.'

'Sure,' Belinda agreed. She took the sheaf of pages and left in silence.

'Morning, Jock,' Belinda said cheerfully, in the common-room an hour later.

'Morning, Belinda. And I must say, you're a treat for sore eyes this morning.'

'Thanks,' she smiled. No wonder, when I dressed specially to please you and your colleagues, she added to herself. She'd borrowed the attractive but subdued blue cotton dress from Charmian, and restricted her accessories to a yellow scarf at the neck.

'Glad I've caught you. I wanted a quick word about Sandie, if I might.'

'Sure. Shall we sit over here?'

They claimed a corner table. 'I gave her your message about the vacancies in the tennis team,' Professor Watson went on, 'and she's definitely interested, but Alice and I weren't sure that she's quite up to the standard. I meant to ask you. . .'

'Ask away.'

He did. And Belinda listened, and considered, and advised. The room was steadily filling up, and she was perfectly happy to keep sitting next to Professor Watson in the corner. And to guide the conversation unobtrusively from his daughter Sandie and the tennis club, to Graham and the golf club—and then, casually, almost in a throwaway manner, to a passing mention of Howard's draft.

There he was, slipping through the door. He poured himself some coffee, and glanced around for a seat.

Belinda tried to catch his eye, but she guessed that he'd avoid her—as he generally did, especially when she was chatting to one of his colleagues.

'Ah,' Professor Watson said, 'speak of the devil.' He got to his feet and called out across the room to Howard.

Howard blanched, but he had little choice but to obey the summons.

'We were talking about you—in the nicest possible way,' Belinda said gaily.

'Belinda was just saying your first draft's almost ready now, Howard. If you'd like me to give it a glance, I've some time to spare on Friday?'

'Well, that would be——'

'Fine, just drop it on my secretary's desk. Now I must be off to my eleven o'clock meeting, so I'll leave you to your gorgeous assistant. Which reminds me, Belinda. If you were thinking of staying with us permanently, there'll be a vacancy coming up in September. You ought to have a word with Mrs Atkins.'

'I'll do that.' Belinda grinned at him. 'And I'll give Sandie a call this evening, I promise.'

'Hobnobbing with the big boss?' Howard asked, half jokingly, half accusingly, as he claimed the chair Professor Watson had just vacated.

'Oh, just chatting about this and that.'

'Nice of him.'

'He's a nice guy. Old friend of Graham's, actually—we're supposed to be having him and his wife to dinner on Saturday week. I don't suppose you'd like to come?'

Howard banged his cup down on the table. 'Belinda, if you think I want you interfering——'

'Howard,' Belinda continued, ruthlessly interrupting him, 'all right, I pushed, but only the tiniest bit. You could see he wasn't offended in the slightest. And I'm doing it for you. Well, for us, really.'

Howard swallowed his words and stared at her.

'It really does help to be on friendly terms with your bosses, you know. And Jock's such a dear; he's like a big bumbling bear. You'd really like him if you got to know him better. Patrick Johnson's even nicer, and—you know, you've got such a good lot of workmates.'

'But asking him to read my draft!'

'He was only waiting to be asked, darling. He's thrilled about your book; he reckons it'll be a big boost to the Unit's reputation. He didn't realise so much of it was already drafted, he said, or he'd have suggested reading it sooner. But now he says he'd love to read it, and maybe give it a mention at that conference in Scarborough he's going to next month.'

'The International Botanists' Convention! But that's just about the biggest——'

'So Jock was saying,' Belinda agreed innocently.

Howard's indignation subsided, his shoulders fell, and he slumped back in his seat. 'I'd never have thought of asking him to do that.'

'I didn't ask him straight out, love. I just guided the conversation around to the possibility.'

'You're so good at that kind of thing,' he muttered.

'Well, I may be a lousy botanist, but I do have my uses, darling.'

Howard didn't reply. She glanced across at him, pleased and yet uneasy: she didn't want to overdo it. After weeks of patient digging away, she could hardly expect him to be persuaded in one morning. But Jennifer had been right, and she was getting there!

'Don't your parents do that kind of thing for each other?' she asked gently.

'Good God, no!'

'Mine do, all the time. I always thought that was what being a couple was all about. Working as a partnership, making plans together, doing things for each other, making sure you both have a good time.'

Silence, broken only by the clatter of coffee-cups around them.

'I've been a blind fool, haven't I?' Howard said in a low, empty voice.

'No, darling,' Belinda replied softly. 'We've both had to do a lot of learning. And we're both still doing it.'

'But I——'

'Better go and get on with Chapter Six,' Belinda said more briskly, putting her cup down and getting to her feet. 'I'll be back in my office if you need me.'

It took all her will-power not to look round as she reached the door of the common-room. She didn't look round as she went up the stairs and along the corridor. She went into the small office she had been allocated, switched on her word processor, sat down, and relocated the page she'd been working on.

It was almost a quarter of an hour later when she heard a gentle knock on the door.

'Come in!' she called out.

Howard came through the door. He closed it behind him and leaned against the inside, heavily.

'Is something up?' asked Belinda.

'Us,' he said quietly. 'You and me.'

'Oh. That.' Her mouth had suddenly gone dry.

'I've been so rotten to you. By all rights you ought to have given up on me months ago,' he said with sudden vehemence.

'Not that rotten. Remember the flowers you sent me?

Anyway——' she licked her lips nervously '——you've been moving in the right direction.'

'I'm just about there now.'

'Are you?'

She was hardly aware of herself standing up, only of Howard striding across the couple of paces that separated them, setting his hands on her shoulders, drawing her to him.

The grey of his eyes was clouded with worry, but somewhere inside them a spark seemed to have ignited into flame.

'We make a great team, don't we?' he said gruffly.

'The best,' she whispered.

'Better think about making it permanent, then.'

'You're sure? I mean,' she went on in a nervous rush, 'I really do have dreadful taste, even if I try to hide it. I'm ever so keen on Kylie Minogue's new single, you know.'

'Are you?' His brows lowered just for an instant, then raised again, his face lightening. 'Then maybe,' he went on, his voice tinged now with laughter, 'you'd better play it for me when we get home!'

· HARLEQUIN · HISTORICAL

CHRISTMAS

· STORIES · 1992 ·

Capture the magic and romance of Christmas in the 1800s
with HARLEQUIN HISTORICAL CHRISTMAS STORIES
1992—a collection of three stories by celebrated
historical authors. The perfect Christmas gift!

Don't miss these heartwarming stories, available in
November wherever Harlequin books are sold:

MISS MONTRACHET REQUESTS by Maura Seger
CHRISTMAS BOUNTY by Erin Yorke
A PROMISE KEPT by Bronwyn Williams

Plus, this Christmas you can also receive a FREE
keepsake Christmas ornament. Watch for details in all
November and December Harlequin books.

DISCOVER THE ROMANCE AND MAGIC OF THE
HOLIDAY SEASON WITH HARLEQUIN HISTORICAL
CHRISTMAS STORIES!

A PLACE IN HER HEART...

Somewhere deep in the heart of every grown woman is the little girl she used to be....

In September, October and November 1992, the world of childhood and the world of love collide in six very special romance titles. Follow these six special heroines as they discover the sometimes heart-wrenching, always heartwarming joy of being a Big Sister.

Written by six of your favorite Superromance authors, these compelling and emotionally satisfying romantic stories will earn a place in your heart!

SEPTEMBER 1992

#514 NOTHING BUT TROUBLE—Sandra James
#515 ONE TO ONE—Marisa Carroll

OCTOBER 1992

#518 OUT ON A LIMB—Sally Bradford
#519 STAR SONG—Sandra Canfield

NOVEMBER 1992

#522 JUST BETWEEN US—Debbi Bedford
#523 MAKE-BELIEVE—Emma Merritt

AVAILABLE WHEREVER
HARLEQUIN SUPERROMANCE
BOOKS ARE SOLD

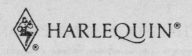
HARLEQUIN®

THE TAGGARTS OF TEXAS!

Harlequin's Ruth Jean Dale brings you
THE TAGGARTS OF TEXAS!

Those Taggart men—strong, sexy and hard to resist...

You've met Jesse James Taggart in FIREWORKS!
Harlequin Romance #3205 (July 1992)

Now meet Trey Smith—he's THE RED-BLOODED YANKEE!
Harlequin Temptation #413 (October 1992)

Then there's Daniel Boone Taggart in SHOWDOWN!
Harlequin Romance #3242 (January 1993)

And finally the Taggarts who started it all—in LEGEND!
Harlequin Historical #168 (April 1993)

Read all the Taggart romances!
Meet all the Taggart men!

Available wherever Harlequin books are sold.